To Kristine

AREA 51
DELETED CHAPTERS
AND OUTTAKES

Access Denied!

Helena
Hunting

COPYRIGHT

OUTTAKE AND
DELETED SCENE

(BECAUSE THERE WAS JUST TOO MUCH LOVING)

Why didn't this gem make the cut?

There were a few significant changes near the end of the story, and with that came the cutting of this scene. Not because I didn't love it, because I do, but there were already plenty of sexy times, and this one just didn't fit into the story anymore. This is another one of those silly scenes I loved, so I'm glad I get to share it in an outtake. This scene takes place in Violet's apartment and the Area 51 debate is in full effect here.

THE LOST SEX SCENE BEAVER FILES

Alex wants to shower with me, but I need private time; the beave requires some 'scaping. No one should see her in such an unruly state but me. He stands outside the door, knocking every few minutes to see if I've changed my mind about needing some help. He's still in the hall when I come out with my robe on. He looks me up and down wearing his pouty face, then brushes by me to take a shower of his own. I don't offer to help him out. We have all night to do that.

While he cleans up, I check the cupboards. I have plenty of snack food, but I only have one box of Kraft mac 'n' cheese, which Alex can polish off on his own, so ordering in seems like the better plan. Since my apartment is close to my work, I know of a few restaurants, but I don't have their phone numbers. Thankfully, Alex's laptop is on the kitchen table—he brought it along so he could check his email later—I'm not sure when he thinks he'll have time since I plan to keep him busy with sexing.

I flip it open and Alex's email pops up. He has a ridiculous number of unanswered messages. I minimize the screens to get to his desktop, which is rife with folders. I spot one called "BEAVER."

I suspect it has nothing to do with the furry animal, and everything to do with porn. I check over my shoulder. For what purpose, I'm not entirely certain. I can hear the water running in the bathroom, and no one else is in my apartment. Maybe I'm awaiting the arrival of the folder-hacking fairy? She hasn't

2

shown up to reprimand me for what I'm about to do yet, so I click on the folder like the nosy pseudo-hacker I am.

Inside the main folder are an assload of dated subfolders. The first one I click contains recent pictures of Alex and me making out in public. I smile, then remember his mother has probably seen them on social media by now. Still, I feel better knowing that he, too, has a porn folder of us.

The next subfolder is called "Beaver Sleuth." I go ahead and click on that. These aren't media pictures. They were taken a few years ago when Skye and Sidney decided we needed to go on a family vacation. It was the off-season, so Buck tagged along. He found a group of dickheads to hang out with on the first day, and all they did was hit on me—the dickheads, not Buck. That would've been weird. Regardless, it was quite the experience. But that's neither here nor there. What I want to know is how Alex happened upon copies of these pictures.

As I browse the folder, I come across one where my butt cheek is hanging out the bottom of my bikini. I was so pissed at Buck for catching me like that, and now Alex has seen it. Not that he hasn't seen my ass up close and personal many, many times, I just don't understand why he feels the need to have old pictures of it peeking out for the world to see. He can have the real thing any time he wants.

I'm so engrossed in checking out my own partially exposed rear end, I don't hear Alex come out of the bathroom. It's not until his hard-on is pressed up against my back that I realize two things: I'm creeping on his computer, and I didn't put real clothes on after my shower—so I'm still naked under my bathrobe.

"Watcha lookin' at?"

He mutters an expletive as he rests his chin on my shoulder. Interestingly, his immediate reaction is to grab my boobs, as though they're my eyes and he's trying to prevent me from seeing what's on the screen.

"It's not what it looks like," he says quickly.

"So this isn't a picture of me with my butt hanging out? Did you get this from Buck? What's he still doing with them anyway, and why in the world would he share them with you?" I try to turn around, but Alex keeps me pinned against the table with the weight of his hips and the monster cock.

"He didn't share them with me."

I glare at his hands, which are anxiously kneading my breasts. "You have three seconds to start explaining before I kick your ass. And don't bother telling me I can't kick your ass. I know that. But I'll lay a smackdown on the monster cock. I have a feeling he's the mastermind behind all of this...this...butt porn." I push my ass out against his monster cock. My boyfriend is such a pervert. Mostly I love it.

"Back up," I order.

Alex complies, and I spin around, crossing my arms over the girls. This is so I look angry, which I am, but also to cover my awesome rack. I don't want any distractions while he explains why he has ass porn photos of me from well before we met each other.

"Remember when we first had sex?" he asks.

I jab a finger into his solid chest. "Don't try to distract me with sex!"

"I'm not! I'm not! But you do remember, right? The first time and the second?" His left dimple makes a brief appearance before he smartly schools his expression.

"Of course I remember." That night, while not my best in terms of decision making, was amazing. It's why we're standing here. And we love each other.

"So you also remember how you took off without waking me up first and didn't call me back after I left you messages?"

Dear God, we aren't going here again, are we? For a famous guy, Alex has a soft ego.

"I told you why I didn't call you back."

He takes my jabbing finger in his hand. "Now don't get mad at me." The precursor to his coming explanation can't be good.

"I was getting desperate to talk to you. I mean, you'd left your glasses behind. I thought that meant you wanted to see me again, but then you didn't call back. I thought maybe I'd done something wrong. I wanted to see you. I was—you were on my mind constantly."

We've never talked about what happened after the first beaver-wood intro. "Really?"

"Yeah. You're this incredibly funny, sexy woman who liked that I was smart and didn't give a rat's ass about hockey. How could I not be taken with you? So when you didn't call me back, I resorted to—" He bites his lip and looks down. "—creeping Buck's Facebook profile."

"You hacked into it?"

"No. I just creeped it. There's where I found the pictures."

"Wait. What? Those pictures are still on his profile? I told him to take them down two years ago."

"I guess he didn't listen. He really should have. Those pictures are something else. I didn't know when you'd be at another game, or if you even wanted to see me again. You told me you loved my cock, so how could I not want to see you again after that?" Alex gets a wistful, faraway look before he continues. "When I saw the picture with your little cheek hanging out, I thought to myself, *Self, you've already seen that fine ass up close and personal. You've held onto it while she rides your cock. You know how soft that skin feels. Is it that wrong for you to keep one picture of Violet's ass cheek playing peekaboo?*" He stops rambling to see how I'm taking his truth vomit.

"For what purpose would you need a picture like that?"

"So I have something to look at while I whack off." He says this like it should be obvious, which I suppose maybe it should.

"You whack off to the pictures in this folder?" I thumb over my shoulder at the computer. I should be angry, maybe even concerned about how sketchy Alex was at the beginning of our relationship. My beaver, however, is already very interested in the visual of Alex stroking his monster cock.

Alex, like the massive, horny pervert he is, must sense my sudden arousal, because he moves in a little closer. "Do you want to see my favorites?"

"I guess?" It's a question. I'm not one-hundred percent on this.

Alex adjusts himself through his towel. "I'm sorry I saved them, but only the ones from Buck. The rest I'm not sorry about at all." He kisses me, all soft-like. "They got me through the weeks when I couldn't see you, or touch you, or be inside of you."

He's good at the sweet talk. I would formulate a response, but I'm too busy with the mouth-fucking.

His lips move to my neck, and he turns me to face the computer again. I can feel Alex's MC nestled against my ass through layers of terry and my robe. He clicks the cursor, opening the subfolder labeled "JACK." Ironically, I have a folder called "JILL" on my own laptop.

Inside, Alex has a ridiculous number of pictures of my cleavage. Many of them appear to have come from his cell phone, based on the photo quality. He must sneak a lot of pictures when I'm not paying attention. He's captured me in the Waters shirt and panties—the ones with WATERS' ASS stamped on the butt. I remember that occasion well. Alex wouldn't let me put pants on to watch the movie, and it ended up being a non-issue since I lost the underwear ten minutes into the flick. Just before they disappeared, he snapped a pic—while I was bent over in front of him, apparently.

"I have a nice ass," I say snarkily.

"It's better than nice," Alex agrees.

"It's still a no-go zone," I warn.

"Oh, I know that, baby. Your ass is far too nice to violate with this." He presses his hips forward so I can feel how hard the MC is.

He makes it sound so damn dirty. For a moment I entertain

the idea that maybe we could—no way. It'll never happen. Ever. That thing does damage to my cooter if I'm not prepped enough, which has only happened once. I can't fathom the trauma if he tried to get it into my Area 51.

My beaver-drooling kicks up a notch at the soft sound of Alex's towel hitting the floor. We're so going to do it in my kitchen, likely on my table.

"This needs to come off, please." He pulls the tie on my robe and tugs on the sleeves. It pools at my feet on the floor. Alex skims my sides and exhales a soft groan. "This is going to be fucking fantastic."

His monster cock slides along my "access denied" crack when he leans against me.

"Alex!" I protest, but I'm also moaning, so it lacks true conviction.

"I'm just making some room." He reaches over me and pushes the laptop to the middle of the table. Once it's out of the way, he runs a hand up my spine. His palm settles between my shoulder blades. "Lean over please, baby."

I do what he asks, even though I'm not sure about what he's got planned. He backs away so the monster cock is no longer making contact. His hands travel along the outsides of my thighs.

"What're you doing?" I crane around to look at him. It's awkward.

"Deciding how exactly I want to have you."

Alex's fingers curl around the back of my knee as he lifts my leg up and to the side. My first reaction is to resist. "Relax, Violet. I'm going to take care of you like I always do."

This is true. He always takes great care of me. So I stop resisting and rest my cheek against the table.

"That's better." He sets my knee on the wood surface, as though I'm climbing over the edge. The angle should be conducive for excellent penetration, as well as a fantastic view for him. It would seem he's all about visual stimulation tonight.

7

"I've wanted to do this since the first night you stayed over. Except I thought we'd be doing it on my kitchen island." He strokes along the back of my thigh. "This is good, though. Maybe when you finally move in with me, I'll do you like this again."

I shiver at his dark tone. "That sounds like a great idea."

"You can move in whenever you want."

A moment later, he bites my right ass cheek. I gasp and then moan as he licks from my beaver button to penetration station. After some well-orchestrated teasing, during which I moan like a professional porn star, his thumb brushes my clit, followed by his tongue.

"You want me to make you come?" he asks.

Obviously I do, but I still tell him what he wants to hear. "That'd be so awesome."

He chuckles against my skin and keeps up with the licking. It's another endless minute until his fingers find their way inside me. It takes less time than that for me to fall apart, muttering profanities about my love for all his moving appendages.

I push up on unsteady arms, groping blindly for his erection.

Alex thwacks me on the ass with his dick. "Is this what you're looking for?"

My protest over the cock-spank is short-lived. Alex moves into position, and slides on in.

"I like this table," I groan as he hits the perfect spot with each thrust.

"Me, too. I especially like eating you on it. Maybe tomorrow I'll have you for breakfast."

My answer is a moan, because I'm totally down with that idea. Sometimes he's a smooth motherpucker.

His hands are on my hips as he pulls out slowly and fills me even more slowly. "How's this? Does it feel good?"

I love how courteous Alex is as a lover, although I think he also likes to hear me say dirty things during sex. Regardless, I'm happy to give him affirmation for the orgasms he provides in abundance.

"More." I want more speed, more friction, more of him.

"You're already taking all of me, baby. More what?" He increases the pace a little.

I arch my back. "More cock."

Alex groans, deep and guttural. "That's just—" Then he fucks me faster and harder, making the table groan with each thrust.

Damn right, *that's just*. The change of angle means he hits that spot inside that makes me see unicorns jumping over rainbows. The porno moans get louder. He's like a jackrabbit. When I come, it's hard. I hold onto the edge of the table for dear life. From what I can tell, Alex has lots of stamina left before he throws in the towel. He slows down, though, giving me time to recover from the orgasm roller coaster. When he picks up the pace again, I feel another orgasm tingling my beaver button. My groan must give me away.

"I'm almost there; wait for me, baby."

What? He wants me to wait for him? How the hell do I do that? I squeeze the beaver, hoping it will postpone my orgasm. I don't have much hope of holding out, though, because I don't know how to do that in the first place.

I begin to protest, but my words catch in my throat at the feel of his fingers on either side of his giant cock. More distracting is the finger perilously close to my backdoor. When it comes in contact with my no-go zone, I moan instead of yell at him and involuntarily push back against him. What the hell? That's not supposed to happen. Alex must take this as a green light. I feel an odd, foreign pressure and then—sweet lord—I come so hard everything goes white.

"That is so fucking sexy," Alex says as he thrusts into me, over and over and over again.

He hasn't even come yet, and worse, if he keeps it up, I'm going to come again. And I do, just as he stills.

Once his body parts are no longer invading mine, I wobble

around to face him, working to remain indignant. "You!" I shake an unsteady finger in his face. "No access. Not allowed, and you—"

"You didn't like it?" Alex catches me in his arms and sets me on the table.

"That's not the point!" So what if I liked it? "I specifically told you that wasn't a place to be putting your parts."

"So you did like it." He smirks.

"I hate you." I smack his chest weakly.

"You love me." He wraps me up in him.

"Whatever." I will not admit I liked what he just did.

"I won't do it again if you don't want me to. I just thought I'd try..." He kisses my temple, all soft and sweet. "I don't expect to ever get anything in there other than a finger or maybe two."

Damn him.

"Fine."

THE HOLIDAY OUTTAKE: CHRISTMAS STYLE

I wrote this piece as a special holiday surprise. It was supposed be about a thousand words, but Alex had a lot to say, and well, Violet engaged in some serious sewing, so I owed it to them to let the scene play out a little longer. Get ready for some Super MC costume changes.

COMING DOWN THE CHIMNEY!

ALEX

I toss my gym bag directly into the laundry room before I head down the hall. I don't do it because I'm anal; it's so Violet doesn't trip over it when she's leaving for work in the morning. I'm not sure how it happens exactly, because it's a huge black duffle bag on a tan tile floor, but she's managed to bruise the crap out of her knees a couple of times and sprain her wrist once.

I don't need her injured over the holidays. Not with her parents coming to visit at the end of next week. Mine will be here, too. We're hosting the family gathering, because I have the space.

Violet's insisted on cooking a turkey, but she's definitely no chef. I'm not sure she realizes how much work is involved in preparing Christmas dinner. My mom will be here to help, so Violet should be fine, but my mom likes to be the master of her own domain. I'm hopeful it won't cause friction between them, and that it won't make it difficult for me to achieve my own friction while they're here.

Violet isn't particularly quiet during sex. Usually I love how vocal she is. But I may have to invest in some kinkery if we're going to have sex with my parents staying here. Like a gag. Even with the spare bedroom all the way down the hall, there's no guarantee they won't hear. Plus my dad's a nighthawk. And he's always got the munchies.

As I enter the kitchen, I'm greeted by the smell of vanilla and char. A tray of star-shaped cookies sits on the island. They're a little dark around the edges, but they don't look too bad. Until I flip one over. It's black on the bottom. I smile and drop it back on the tray. She's making an effort. It's cute.

"Violet, baby? Where are you?" I check the main floor, but there's no sign of her. Since her car is in the garage—the one I bought her. Because I can. And I want to—I assume she's upstairs.

Tomorrow morning I leave for a series of away games. I'll be gone a week, and when I get back, my sister and her best friend will be in town and likely hanging out with us a lot. That means our usual "Welcome Home Fuck Day" routine, as Violet so sweetly dubbed it, may not be easy to pull off. We'll see. My plan is to get as much action as I can tonight, as many ways as I can get it, so I'm stocked up for the time away.

I hit the stairs, taking them two at a time. "Baby? I'm home," I call. Still, I'm met with silence. Where the hell is she?

I rearrange my hard-on so it's not at a weird angle and head toward our bedroom, picturing her naked in the shower, or better yet, in the tub. Now I'm all excited. Workouts do that to me; all the exertion without any follow-up release can be tough to take. Much like away games.

I push open the door and cross to the bathroom, expecting to find her lying in the Jacuzzi tub, surrounded by bubbles, her gorgeous, long auburn hair piled up high on her head. I can already see her luscious, awesome tits bobbing in the water. But there's nothing. What the fuck?

I return to the hall. All the doors are open, the way Violet likes them. She gets weirded out when she can't see what's going on behind them. The one at the end of the hall, which is Violet's private space—and mostly where she keeps all the crap she doesn't want to throw away but doesn't know where to put—is shut up tight.

She's been hiding out in there a lot. I'm starting to get concerned about it, to be honest. We've only been living together for four months, but we're coming up on a year since we started dating. You learn a lot about a person over twelve months. I hope the amount of time she's been spending in her "office" isn't a sign that things aren't as awesome as I think.

With that in mind, I creep toward her room. A creaky spot in the floor makes me pause, but music seeps through the door, the bass vibrating. I put my hand on the knob and turn. But it's locked.

What's she doing in there that would warrant locking the door? What's she hiding from me? I put my ear against the wood and hear a low hum. It's steady and repetitive—like a vibrator. Now I really want to get in there.

We have great sex. All the time. Constantly. Even when I'm away, I call her and we phone fuck. God, I love phone fucking. I love the way Violet sounds like she's right there with me. I love it when she tells me she misses my cock. And now she's locked herself in her office with her vibrator where I can't get to her.

I knock, probably with more force than I need to. A little shriek of surprise follows, and the vibrator stops humming.

"Violet? Why's the door locked?" I rattle the knob.

"Hold on! I'll be right there."

It sounds like things are being knocked over. "If you're naked, don't bother getting dressed." I draw my shirt over my head and run a hand through my hair. Then I pull my belt free from the loops and pop the top button on my jeans. Just so I'm prepared.

Violet peeks out through a crack. "Hi, baby!" Her single eye darts down over my bare chest to my open pants. "Oh, hey." She opens the door a little more and slides out of the narrow gap.

Most of Violet is small, apart from her boobs. Those are not small. She cringes as she mashes them against the jamb, trying to get through without opening the door any wider. She's definitely hiding something. I take in her outfit. She's wearing her robe, the red one with my team logo on it. It's the middle of the afternoon.

"Were you jilling off in there?" It comes out snappy.

Her eyebrows furrow. "What?"

"Why are you wearing this? What were you doing in there?" I try to push past her, but she bars the way with a hand on either side of the doorway. I can easily move her aside. She weighs half of what I do. But I should give her a chance to explain before I go barging into what's supposed to be her personal space.

"I'm making your Christmas present."

"What?" I'm confused. The humming sound, her state of semi-dress, and the flush in her cheeks all lead me to believe she's been petting her pussy. "But I heard a vibrator."

"Vibrator?"

"Yeah."

"That was my sewing machine, baby." Violet pulls the door closed behind her. Then she puts her hands on my bare chest. "I only use my vibrator when you're not here to provide your extensive sexual services, Alex. You know that." She bites her lip and leans in, her boobs rubbing against my stomach. I'm not sure if this is meant as a distraction or not.

I glance down. Her robe is satin, the deep V gaping. She rises up on her toes and kisses the bottom of my chin. "And even if I did need to jill off, why would I bother doing it in my office? We have a very spacious, comfortable bed. If I'm going through all the effort in the first place, me and Buddy are doing it lying down."

I tense. Buddy is her vibrator. At first I thought it was funny. It's a battery-operated dick that looks like a beaver wearing tightie whities. His name is literally Buddy the Beaver. When I'm not home and she has to manage on her own, she tells me Buddy's in bed with her. It drives me fucking nuts.

"You were worried." It's not a question.

I nod. Sometimes it works in my favor to be sensitive. Violet loves that I can kick the shit out of someone on the ice—not that I need to, or do very often—but then I come home and I'm all

15

soft and warm and cuddly. And sometimes I'm a little needy. Like right now. Because I'm leaving in the morning.

I'm not going to sleep beside her. See her. Touch her. Be inside her. The long stretches are the worst.

"You know you're my number one." She slips her arms around my neck and tugs.

Her mouth tastes like candy canes. I don't have much patience. We have hours, but it doesn't feel like enough time. I pick her up, and she wraps her legs around my waist. I hold on to her ass and carry her to our bedroom.

Her lips are on my neck, traveling up to my ear. "I had a nap this afternoon. I figured the Super MC might want to have a little party with my beaver."

This lifts some of the heaviness of my mood. I chuckle and nuzzle her throat, pushing the door open. When I reach the bed, I drop her on the comforter. She scooches back, making room, and I grab her ankles to keep her from getting too far. Joining her on the bed, I kneel between her parted legs, skimming along her calves up to her knees.

Violet leans back on her elbows, watching me. Her lips are parted, her long hair hanging down to brush the bed. I'm trying to decide what I want to do first. If I fuck her mouth, I can recover while I lick her pussy. Or I could start with eating her, and then we can have sex, and I can get the blow job later. So many options. So few hours to cover them all.

Violet drags a finger along the edge of her robe, where the loose V dips at her cleavage. Or we could start with tit-fucking, which inevitably means my dick will end up in her mouth. I kiss the inside of her knee, then run my hands up her thighs. Violet's hips lift, seeking out the touch I've yet to provide. I feel like teasing. And maybe getting what I want first. I pull the tie on her robe, setting the two sides free. The satin slides over her hips, revealing a whole lot of *what the fuck*.

She's wearing only a bra and panties. But it's what's going on with the panties that has me stopping.

"Oh, shit!" She grabs her robe and pulls it closed. She tries to do the same with her knees, but I hold them open with my palms.

"What's going on down here?"

"You're not supposed to see! It's part of the surprise!"

"What surprise?"

"Your Christmas present. Damn it. You distracted me, and I forgot I was wearing these." She motions to her crotch, which she's covered. All I've gotten is a glimpse so far, and I'm not exactly sure what I was looking at.

I reach out with the intention of pushing her hands away so I can see better.

"No, Alex! Don't! You'll ruin my surprise!"

She does some weird flailing thing, like she's attempting a backwards somersault, but she's not managing it very well. I let go of her, and she rolls to the side. Turning away from me, she quickly loses her panties and tosses them on the floor. She struggles with her bra, but I don't bother to help, just in case that's part of the surprise as well. The red satin of her robe slides over her shoulders, revealing her narrow waist and then goes lower.

She looks over her shoulder at me just as she reveals the dimples above her ass. And then it pools around her body on the comforter. "Are you planning to fuck me until I can't walk, Alex?"

My eyes shoot up to hers. She's referencing the time we had sex in the locker room after I was ejected from a game for fighting. It was a bad place to get it on, but God, that sex is cemented in my spank bank Hall of Fame for the rest of my life. It's my go-to jack-off material when I'm away.

Instead of tackling Violet to the bed, I move her hair over her shoulder and kiss her neck. "Is that what you were hoping for?"

"If all I'm getting for the next week is Buddy, then yes, please."

This time when I kiss her neck, I use teeth. Glancing over her shoulder, I look down at her breasts. Her nipples are hard, as they should be. I reach around and palm one. With my other hand I push my jeans and boxers over my hips, setting my cock free. I pull her to me, rubbing my dick against her ass.

She tenses for a second, then moans when I caress her other breast and thumb her nipples. Violet gets a little antsy when my dick's near her ass. I think she thinks I'm just going to try to slip it in there one day. I might be able to do that with a finger, which I've only managed once so far, but my cock isn't a slip-in kind of appendage.

After close to a year, Violet still requires a primer before sex, otherwise it's too much and I end up putting her out of commission for a couple of days. Which is no good. Especially on a night like tonight.

My cock settles in its natural spot, the cleft of her ass. "Alex," Violet warns.

"Don't worry, baby, your ass is safe." I slide a hand down her stomach.

"You say that, but I think Super MC has other ideas."

"He knows there are other tight, warm places he gets to hang out in."

She turns around in my arms, leaning back so my cock sticks straight out at her. "You mean my belly button?" She thrusts her stomach forward and tries to get the head to hit her navel, but she misses by a couple inches.

"That hole's way too small." I'm about to grab hold of her again when I notice, aside from how awesome her boobs look, that she's got black lines on her stomach and under her boobs. They leave a smudge when I rub them. "What's this?"

She looks down. "Oh. Uh…I was making a pattern, and this seemed like the easiest way to ensure it was going to work."

"What kind of pattern?"

"It's part of the surprise." She leans into me, her boobs mashing against my chest. "Stop trying to ruin your Christmas present."

"You know, you might want to give it to me early." I run my hands down her sides, pulling her hips to mine so I can rub my hard-on against her stomach.

"Why would I want to do that?" Violet tilts her head back, and I kiss her neck.

"My sister's going to be here when I get back, and Lily's coming with her, then my parents the next day." I keep up with the slow, wet kisses. "We won't have a lot of privacy over the holidays. We could have an early celebration. I already picked up one of your gifts." I pull back. "We could do an exchange, and you could show me what you made for me."

Violet gives me the eye. "You have zero patience."

I trail a finger down her stomach, circling her navel and going lower, I stop before I get to her bare pussy. I give her what she calls my pouty-sexy face. I'd be offended, because I don't think I pout, but I do whatever gets me what I want. "Just one little present? We're going to have a house full of people, Violet. What if we don't have time to enjoy whatever it is you're making?"

She sighs. It makes her boobs jiggle. "Okay, fine." She pushes on my chest. "Lie down and wait here. I'll be right back."

I do as I'm told, pushing the covers down and reclining against the pillows as Violet hops off the bed, grabs her panties and robe from the floor, and runs out of the bedroom.

Christmas is my favorite holiday. I was that kid who used to find my parents' hiding spot for presents and carefully open every package. I always knew what I was getting before I got it. Sunny refused to join me in the game, but she never ratted me out. She figured if I wanted to ruin my own surprises that was on me, as long as I didn't ruin hers.

I bought Violet her own pair of skates. Good ones. So she can learn, because she still doesn't know how. I got her a couple other things, but the skates are the fun gift. Though probably not as fun as what she has planned.

I tuck my hands behind my head and wait. And wait some

more. And a little more. My hard-on's deflating. "Violet, baby? You coming back any time soon?"

"One more minute!"

One more minute turns into several. By this time I'm almost all the way soft again. I'm about to get up when she struts into the room wearing a pair of sparkly red heels. Well, *struts* is probably the wrong word.

Violet's not great in high heels. She can do ones she calls kittens, but these are hooker heels—super tall with a platform. Her red satin robe is tied at the waist with a white ribbon. She's wearing an elf hat, and she has a red drawstring bag slung over one shoulder. It's sexy as fuck, even if she's struggling with the walking part. She takes her time shuffling over to me. She almost rolls her ankle, and I spring up, ready to grab her, but she recovers, grabbing the post at the end of the bed like it was intentional.

She climbs over the footboard, the gap in her robe showing off her ample cleavage. My hard-on is back like magic. She tosses the red bag on the bed, and I reach for it, but she slaps my hand. "No peeking!"

I hold my hands up in apology, then drop them by my sides, waiting to see what she's going to do next. She seems pretty excited about whatever it is she has planned.

Still wearing the robe, Violet straddles my hips and settles over my cock. The satin brushes my legs and falls on my abs. The head of my cock peeks out. I don't move, too entertained by the flush in her cheeks and the way she's gripping the hem together at the bottom.

I'm trying to discern all the sensations. The heat is damp, almost verging on wet, which isn't unusual for Violet. She's slippery when she's excited. There's another sensation, though, soft and foreign. I slide my palms up her legs, but she stops them before I get too far. Threading her fingers through mine, she leans forward and kisses my chin, then my lips.

"Be patient, baby."

"I'm trying. I've been waiting to get inside you all day."

She grins. "Not long now, and you'll be jumping down the chimney."

"What?"

Her eyebrows rise, but that's all the answer I get. She pushes away, sitting up. "Ready?"

"For you? Always."

She gives me a cheeky wink, adjusts her elf hat, then swings her leg over so she's no longer straddling me. Maybe I'm about to get a blow job. She makes a face when she takes in my dick. It's wet. From her pussy. I love that about her. We only need lube for tit fucks.

"Shit. Why am I always so leaky?" She turns her back to me and rubs the hem of her robe on my cock. If she's putting it in her mouth, I don't see the point.

That's not what happens, though. Violet straddles me again, almost stabbing me in the face with one of her heels. I grab her ankle before she can take my eye out, which puts her off balance, and she falls forward, sprawling out over my legs.

"You okay, baby?" I ask.

"Yup. Yeah. Sorry, the heels are a little dangerous. Maybe I need to take them off?" She looks over her shoulder at me, apologetic.

I run my hands up her calves. "Leave them on. I like them, just no sudden movements." I'm all the way hard now. The idea of going at it reverse cowboy helps with that. I love watching Violet's ass jiggle when she's riding my cock from behind. I don't get to do that very often, because she's always afraid I'm going to take advantage of the view.

"Okay." She drops her Santa bag between my legs.

"What's going on over there?"

"You'll see in a minute."

I keep stroking her calves while she does whatever she's doing. I prop myself up on my elbow, trying to get a peek, but she digs her heel into my side.

"Ow!"

She smacks my thigh. "I said no peeking."

I flop back down and decide to be patient. I lift the hem of her robe and check out the sweet view of her ass. She's wearing a thong. I might love Violet's boobs more than anything, but her ass is a close second. She's got this fabulous curvy body with a tiny waist and a luscious, biteable ass. I tuck the robe into the back of her panties and start kneading the supple skin, grazing the divide with my thumbs.

She tenses and shrieks, swatting at my hands. "What are you doing?"

"Entertaining myself."

"Stay away from my Area 51."

"I can't make that kind of promise. You should hurry up with my surprise." I'm joking. Mostly. But it gets a rise out of her.

Violet starts handling my cock. She's not stroking, though. She wraps something around the head and giggles. I feel something cold, then something soft.

"Are you dressing up my dick again?"

She snickers. "Maybe."

"You're not tying anything to him!" I bolt upright, and Violet nearly topples over. The last time she dressed up my dick—as a superhero—she almost decapitated him. The cape she made required a bow, which turned into a knot. Scissors were involved in the removal. It was not my favorite moment.

"I'm using Velcro!"

"You're sticking things to my dick with Velcro?" I wrap an arm around her waist and pick her up. Her heel slides across my abs, leaving behind a red mark, which I'll happily take if she's not suffocating my dick again.

Violet scrambles over my legs, straddling the right way around and tries to cover my cock with her robe. "He's not ready!"

"Seriously, Violet?"

Her shoulders droop and her mouth turns down at the corners, her disappointment obvious.

I sigh. "Fine. Finish what you're doing, but quickly. You're killing my hard-on." I cross my arms over my chest while she produces a tiny Santa hat. She keeps my dick hidden behind her robe. A few seconds later she pulls the satin to the side.

"Voila!" She does jazz hands on either side of my cock. "Santa Dick!"

My cock is indeed dressed up like Santa. She's gone so far as to sew a Santa coat with little stuffed arms and crafted a beard out of what I assume is felt and cotton balls. It's Velcroed under the base of the head. It even has eyes and a nose. A little Santa hat tops the head.

I point to the nose. "Is that a Nerd?"

She nods enthusiastically. "And the eyes are candies too!"

I look up and realize my dick is not the only thing that's dressed up. Mini candy canes hang from Violet's nipples. I think she's taped them there. While that's inventive, it's the underwear I'm most fascinated by. They look like a chimney, with a snowy top, except upside down. I gesture to her crotch. "What's going on here?"

She climbs back into my lap. One of the candy canes falls off her boob. She pauses to reattach it. Then she rises, so the chimney is over top of my slowly deflating Santa dick. He's starting to lean to the right. Violet lowers herself a few inches and the chimney flap covers my dick. The little hat falls off.

"See! Santa's going down the chimney!" She flips up the flap, which she's sewn to the top of the panties to show me. "Do you like it?"

I shake my head and laugh. "You're ridiculous."

"I know." She covers him with the chimney and bobs up and down again, making him disappear and reappear a couple of times.

I let her entertain herself briefly before I make a suggestion. "You should eat the candies now."

Violet tosses one of the candy canes at me before she leans down and sucks the eyes off the head, followed by the Nerd nose.

23

Then she licks her way around, cleaning off the candy adhesive. I groan and slide my fingers into her hair. On the next pass she removes the dick sock/Santa coat and takes in more of me.

I shift her body so her ass faces me, then pull her panties over her hips so I can get her ready. She moans on my cock when I ease two fingers inside her and start pumping. I add one more, just to make sure she's ready before I pull her off and bring her mouth to mine. Violet climbs on top of me and sinks down.

Her elf hat falls off, her long hair tickling my chest as she leans in to brush her lips over mine. "Did you like my surprise?"

"It was very entertaining."

"The Velcro works nice."

"It does." I grip her ass and grind her over me.

"Thanks for letting me dress up your dick."

"Thanks for hugging him when you were done playing dress up."

She giggles. "Vagina hugs are the best, right?"

"Definitely the best."

I'll give Violet her present later. When I'm done providing orgasms.

THE VALENTINE'S DAY LOVE LETTER

Violet,

I hope you're not mad at me for the singing telegram. I thought it was funny, and we have the same whacked out sense of humour, so fingers crossed it went over okay. I figured if it came with candy and flowers you'd be willing to forgive me for embarrassing you in front of your colleagues. If not, I'll just make it up to your boobs, because they always forgive me for the dumb shit I do.

If it's not too much to ask, maybe you could wear the Spiderman jammies tonight? And your glasses. I'm having dinner brought in, because I don't want to share you.

Love,

Alex

PUCKED UP DELETED CHAPTERS

When I started this book, I had a plan, and then I went back and added all this material, and realized it was keeping Miller and Sunny apart for far too long, so I ended up cutting what amounted to a good 10-20k. Some of it was repurposed and added to the story later on, but this chunk just had to go.

I think it showcases just how altruistic Miller really is, and how bad his luck can be. There's also a little Randy, pre-Lily in here, so forgive his behavior please. ;)

CHAPTER ONE

ALTRUISM AIN'T EASY

I smell like a farm animal. I probably look like one, too, based on my lack of access to things like razors and hot water. I might stink worse than my lucky hockey socks during playoffs, and those were rank by the time the finals came around. My housekeeper wouldn't let me keep my hockey bag in my condo anymore because it stunk up the whole place. I didn't think it was that bad, but I moved it to the balcony anyway so she'd stop throwing floral air fresheners in there.

But the reason for my current state of grossness has nothing to do with hockey. Every year, as soon as the official season is over, I spend a few weeks doing volunteer work. Usually it takes me out of the country. It's a break from the city and the intensity of being an NHL player.

For the past ten days, I've been part of the labor crew on a construction project. I'm decent at building things. That and gym were the only classes in high school where I managed to get decent marks. And sometimes I'd do okay in art class if I wasn't goofing off with the sculpting clay.

Today we finally finished our phase of the job. All that's left is the painting and decorating. Another crew is coming to replace us tomorrow, so by the end of the month it should be ready.

The building will house kids who lost their families in the most recent hurricane to rip up Haiti. With twenty-five eight-by-eight bedrooms, a cafeteria with a kitchen, two communal bathrooms, a utility room, and a common room, it's supposed to hold up to a hundred kids. Each tiny bedroom has two bunk beds. The whole place is built for utility, not luxury. A small, shared room is way better than not having a place to sleep at all. Sometimes nature can be assholely to people who didn't have much to begin with.

For the first three days, we slept in tents. It's not the most comfortable, but having done this since I was a teenager, I've learned a good yoga mat helps a lot. After we finished building the first floor, we moved inside. I'm too wide and tall to fit into the bunk beds—they seem like they'd work well for munchkins—so I slept on the floor. These trips always put my cushy life into perspective.

Usually my dad comes with me—he's the one who started taking me in the first place—but he had another trip planned this year, so it's just been me, one other player, and some volunteers. It's been fun for the most part, aside from Randy, my teammate and friend, bitching about the lack of bunnies.

This year I wasn't as excited about going as I usually am. I've been hanging out with a girl, and being out of the country leaves her wide open for dates with someone other than me. I wouldn't be all that worried, but we haven't had a discussion about not seeing other people, and things were kind of up in the air when I left for Haiti.

Anyway, it's been hotter than Satan's steaming jock strap today, and humid. I've been going commando the last couple of days since I ran out of clean underwear. My balls are sticking to the inside of my leg, and the fly of my jeans is chafing my dick. I'd stick my hand down my pants and fix the problem, but there are kids around. I'll manage the discomfort. By this time tomorrow I'll be back in my air-conditioned condo.

Ricardo, one of the local guys who oversaw the project, invited us to his home for a Haitian style BBQ tonight in celebration of completing our work, so that's where we're headed now. It'll be a great end to an exhausting, but rewarding trip.

The aftermath of the hurricane surrounds us as we walk. Trees ripped out by the roots line the side of the road. Other ones are broken in half, the tops folded over. The dirt road, mostly washed out from the flooding, kicks up dust as we go.

I jam my hand in my pocket, feeling for the finger-sized hole in there, hoping to unstick my ball sac from the side of my leg. I'd try to shake it free, but it'll make me look like a dog who's just relieved himself on a tree.

I palm my phone. I've had it with me this entire trip, hoping to run across some kind of reception. But I haven't gotten more than one bar since we arrived—not even in the town they've already partially rebuilt. Once I was almost able to check my messages, but then I lost the signal. My battery's down to twenty percent. We've been using generators to power our drills and skill saws because there isn't any electricity. So there hasn't been a way to charge phones.

That means I haven't had contact with anyone, including my assistant or my sort-of girlfriend. It's a pain in my ass. I have shit to do when I get back to Chicago that I can't plan for. I need my calendar. It might be the off-season, but I'm still busy.

I'm not looking forward to sorting through the mess of emails and messages that will be waiting for me when I get home tomorrow. Worse than the email backlog is that my assistant is going on her own vacation, so I'll have to organize my own life for the next couple of weeks. It's not my strong suit.

We come around a bend in the uneven road, and the trees open to reveal a small hut in the middle of a sparse, grassy patch of land. It almost reminds me of a Hobbit home, except it's not round. The walls are a flat grey, and the roof is made of corrugated metal panels. The whole thing would probably fit in my living room. Outside this tiny house are at least fifty people.

Kids run around, playing with the too-big sticks and rubber balls we brought so we could teach them how to play street hockey. Makeshift nets made of wood scraps and ripped up fishing net sit at both ends of the yard.

The boys are dressed in hand-me-down shirts with American logos. The girls wear boy's basketball shorts and frilly tops with sequins. All of them are covered in dust and grime, and none of them seems to care. It's interesting to be in a place where iPads and devices aren't used as babysitters.

Across the front of the house is a banner that reads "Thank You" in messy, kid-painted scrawl. I turn on my phone and snap a few pictures. Once I get back I'll add them to the project page so the construction company who helped fund the effort along with me and Randy can get some positive recognition.

It's as I'm snapping pictures that the most amazing sight in the world finally registers. On top of the tiny little house with its rusted and definitely not waterproof roof is a giant mofo satellite dish.

"Holy puck!" I've had to do a lot of censoring this week because of all the kids running around. They're everywhere. Kind of like ants, but they're cuter and not annoying.

"Right? Check out the hottie." Randy puts his hand out for a high five.

I'm busy checking for a signal, so I leave him hanging. My phone is at nineteen percent. One bar appears, then a second and a third in the top left corner. I hold the phone up in his face. "I have bars!"

"Really?" He has to back up to see it. "Man! I wish my phone hadn't died three days ago."

"I'mma try to call Sunny while we're here."

"You haven't talked to her this whole time, right? You think that's gonna make things worse?" Randy knows things were a little iffy when I came here.

I shrug instead of respond. I've been trying to get Sunshine Waters, Sunny for short, to date me for the past few months. It sure as hell feels like longer. The problem is she's the sister of one of my teammates, Alex Waters. He's also the team captain. And he's dating my sister, Violet. In fact, they moved in together just before I left for Haiti. I'm not sure it's a great idea, but Vi seems happy. For now. Until he fucks it up.

So far I've been doing a stellar job of fucking things up with Sunny. It's not really my fault. Or maybe it is. I'd prefer to blame it on social media, which does nothing to make things easier.

"You sure it isn't better just to leave things alone? I mean, it'd be way less tense with Waters if you weren't all up in his sister."

"Like he is in mine."

"But you're not really related."

"We've been family for five years."

Ricardo lets out this crazy loud whistle from ten feet in front of us. It nearly blows out my eardrums. It also puts a stop to my conversation with Randy, which is probably good, since it's not a topic I like.

All the kids stop what they're doing. There's a collective shout of excitement, and then we're swarmed. A little girl with two long, dark braids tugs on my arm and shoves a piece of paper with a drawing on it at me. Her voice is squeaky with excitement. I power down my phone and slip it back into my pocket, nodding as she chatters away, explaining the drawing in a language I can't understand. But I don't need to know the words to get that she's looking forward to having a home.

We spend the afternoon playing street hockey with the kids, drinking some kind of homemade wine that tastes like gasoline, and eating. Some of the food, particularly the meat, is unidentifiable. But the kids eat it, and so does everyone else, so I assume it's safe.

Later, the sky takes on a pink haze, and the sun dips below the treeline, creating shadows that creep across the grass. I help the kids find kindling for a fire, which isn't hard with all the broken and damaged trees. We pick out special sticks for marshmallow roasting. I brought a few bags with me, knowing it's a luxury they don't often get. Watching their eyes light up with the excitement that only comes from new experiences is awesome.

I let Randy take care of making the fire since he seems like he's trying to impress one of the women who looks to be about our age. Excusing myself, I slip away to check my phone. Powering it on, I cringe at the sixteen percent battery that's left.

As soon as I take it out of airplane mode, it starts dinging like crazy and it drops another percent. Keying in my passcode, I go to Sunny's messages first. She texted me a few times at the beginning of the week and then again yesterday. Using the text-to-speech app will drain the battery faster, so I struggle my way through reading her shortened text speak.

Message one reads:

> Hope u had a good flite.

Message two reads:

> Checked flite #. Says u landed OK.
> Guess ur busy with wrk alredy.

Messages three takes me a good two minutes to decipher:

> Pls txt bk when u get this. No 1 posts FB.
> Do u have aces? Going 2c Alex 4 2days.

Message four is from yesterday:

> No sure if ur still comin 2c me when u get bk?

I send a reply right away, keeping it short and to the point. I pray it goes through with the spotty two-bar reception.

> Calling u.

I don't wait to hear back before I call. It goes to her voicemail the first time, but she picks up right away on my second attempt.

"Hello?"

"Sunny?"

Static crackles on the line. "Miller?"

"Hey, sweets. I missed your voice."

"How c…from you…week."

The connection isn't great. Half of her words are dropped, and she sounds tinny, but at least I can sort of talk to her. It's way better than trying to figure out her texts.

"We didn't have reception. We didn't even have power most of the week. Everything ran on generators. Ricardo's throwing us a party, and he has this monster satellite dish, so I have two bars. Can you hear me? I can't hear you real good. I don't have a lot of battery left."

She replies, but it's lost in static. I put her on speakerphone and walk around the house, watching the little dots as they go from two down to one and then up to three.

"Sunny Sunshine? You still there?"

"You're at a party? I didn't know… Hockey…Haiti… bunnies…too?"

I may not catch everything she says, but I can tell from her tone she's not happy. She's using sarcasm. Bunnies are the biggest problem for me and Sunny—not my involvement with them as much as the fact that they still call me and hound me in bars and want pictures and stuff.

"It's not that kind of party. It's a BBQ. A bunny-free zone."

"Oh. Okay." There's a slight pause, along with a soft exhale.

"How are things there? Are you having fun?"

"It's been good. Tiring but good. I'm looking forward to being home. And seeing you. It's still cool for me to visit?"

She replies, but I can't hear through the static.

"I missed that."

Ricardo's wife, Mira, taps me on the shoulder. "Mr. Miller? You have sticks?"

"Did someone just ask to see your dick?" Sunny asks.

"No. No. Sticks." Jesus. Bad connections suck almost as much as having no connection at all. "We've been teaching the kids how to play hockey. Tonight we're having a campfire and roasting marshmallows. Did you know most of these kids have never even eaten a marshmallow?"

"Swallow? Swallow what?"

"No. Marshmallow. Not swallow."

"Miller, this is the first time we've talked in ten days and you want to know whether or not I swallow?"

"Oh! Mr. Miller. Is that your wife? She happy to have you home." Mira grabs the phone from me. "Ms. Miller? You lucky woman! Mr. Miller he love the babies. He teach them the hockey." She starts speaking in Haitian, going back to broken English after a few seconds. "He good man. So much the help. And, how you say, the heated? The hottie? Yes, yes. The hottie. You have lots baby and make happy."

She passes back the phone and grabs my hand, looking at my fingers. "No ring?"

"We're dating."

She gives me a questioning look.

"Not married."

"No marry? Why you wait for?"

"We just started dating."

She rolls her eyes and shakes her head, then leaves me alone again.

"Who was that?"

"Ricardo's wife. She doesn't speak a whole lot of English."

"I think I got the gist of it." Sunny sounds more like she's laughing and less like she's still mad at me.

I check my battery. It's dying fast. I'm at three percent. "My phone's gonna cut out soon. I just wanted to call and make sure you still wanna to see me."

"I still want to see you."

"Cool. Awesome. I don't when my flight gets in 'cause I can't check my emails, but I'll call when I have the details."

"Okay. I should let you—"

The call cuts out. I check the screen to find it's gone blank. My phone's officially dead. I'm not worried, though. I get to see Sunny in less than forty-eight hours. Everything just went from good to awesome.

CHAPTER TWO

IT AIN'T NO THING, CHICKEN WING

The moonshine I drank last night may be partially at fault for how I'm feeling. But I don't think it's the whole reason. My stomach gurgles, and a cold sweat breaks out across my forehead as I wait in the line to get my boarding pass. There's no special line for NHL players. Not that I expected there to be, but it's nice when I get VIP treatment, especially when I feel this awful.

I just need to make it through the next hour, and everything will be okay. If I shit my pants before then, they won't let me on the plane back to Chicago. And I don't want to receive medical attention here. For one, I don't speak Haitian. They could take a kidney, and I wouldn't know until I woke up with stitches. I bet they wouldn't even use anesthetic, like in one of those horror movies.

I put the lockdown on those thoughts. They don't help with the nausea.

Before I made the commitment to stand in this line like a chump, I defiled the men's bathroom. I'm positive I'm going to need another toilet timeout before long. It feels like my insides are trying to escape my body, and they can't decide whether they want to come out my ass or my mouth. I have a new respect for what Violet goes through when she eats dairy. The punishment doesn't seem to fit the crime if she experiences anything half as bad as this.

Randy claps me on the back. "You all right, man?"

I grunt. I'm saving all my words for the tiny woman checking passports at the desk. Also, if I speak, I might barf, and I'm back to them not letting me on the plane.

"I think I drank too much last night," Randy mumbles. "It feels like someone's trying to hammer their way through my skull."

Again, I make a noise. I have no idea how much he drank, but there were shots of something after all the kids went to sleep in their various tents. I declined those. I didn't drink half as much as Randy last night, but today I'm feeling much worse than he seems to be.

Maybe it's the "wings" that are causing my stomach issues more than the booze. I'm having a hard time believing they were from chickens because the wild ones I saw running around were way too scrawny to eat. Whatever we consumed, it's coming out today in ways nothing ever should.

Thankfully, the line is moving, so I'll be able to hit the bathroom again soon.

I hand over my passport and flight documents. Randy's chatting up the much younger, much flirtier chick at the next desk, and she's giggling like a teenager. The older, less impressed woman helping me flips open my passport and does a triple take.

I'm clean-shaven in the picture, and four years younger. I weigh about thirty pounds less than I do now—although if I keep it up with the bathroom trips, I might be close to that weight again soon. Right now I'm sporting a serious beard. While the rest of my hair is blond verging on white after being in the sun for the past ten days, my beard is closer to red. Like I'm part ginger, but only on my chin and upper lip. Before the trip, I was well groomed; after ten days without a razor, I look like I'm ready to audition for an episode of *Teen Wolf.*

"Please take off your hat, sir."

My hair's a greasy, disgusting mess since it's been trapped under there all morning, but I do what I'm asked.

She inspects my passport and then me again, typing away on her little computer with a frown. When it's clear I'm not a dangerous felon looking to escape the Haitian prison system, she hands me back my passport.

"Would you like an aisle or a window seat?"

"Is there anything left by the exits?"

"I'm sorry, those seats are already taken."

"Nothing with extra leg room? I'm kinda tall for those standard seats."

"Sorry, sir, I have row twelve, window only, or seats at the back of the plane. Those are close to the restrooms."

I don't want to be too close to the bathroom since I plan to abuse it. I booked the tickets as economy. Randy's in first class, but I felt like a dick flying with the specials to go help people who have nothing. I'm regretting that decision now.

It's a seven-hour flight. I feel like shit. Not only am I in economy, but the back of the plane means getting on and off last. Considering the state of my gut, it's less than ideal. I can't manage seven hours in one of those tiny seats feeling the way I do. It was bad enough on the way here.

I lean on the desk so I'm not quite so imposing, and also my stomach is cramping again. I'm worried I might not make it to a bathroom if we don't hurry things along. I smile and hope it doesn't look like a grimace. "Are there any spots left in business or first class?"

She clicks away on the keyboard with her pale pink nails. They're decorated with tiny flowers on the tips. Sunny's are often pretty like that. I wonder how they do it.

"There are seats available in first class."

I heave a relieved sigh. "That's great."

"There will be a charge of one thousand two hundred and twenty dollars to upgrade."

That's a lot of money to sit in a better seat. But the guilt isn't bad enough to stop me from passing over my credit card to secure my spot among the privileged jerkoffs. The bathroom by first class is less frequented. I'll have extra legroom, and I won't have to sweat all over my neighbor because we won't be sitting on top of each other. To make up for it, I'll donate twice that amount to fund a program at the orphanage when I get home.

Violet, my sister and financial manager, is going to shit a brick when she sees my credit card statements. I think I've gone over budget for this trip by about ten grand. Except for my hangover and possible food poisoning, it's all been for a good cause.

If I have her set up some kind of educational thing for the kids who have trouble learning, she won't be able to fight me on it. School was never about class, but all about sports for me. Later in high school, when my teeth were fixed, it was all about sports and girls. Not much has changed, except that I'm interested in one girl in particular now.

My lack of baggage makes everything go a lot faster once I've got my boarding pass. On the way to Haiti, I checked three suitcases. Coming home all I have are the clothes on my back, a backpack of handmade gifts from the local kids and their families, and a shitload of Imodium—which isn't working at all.

The security check is superfast, thank Christ. I rush to the closest bathroom and give birth to the devil. When I'm done ruining yet another public restroom, I find Randy lounging in one of the uncomfortable chairs at our gate.

Now he looks as bad as I feel. Even still, there's a chick sitting beside him, cozied up like maybe she's thinking about climbing into his lap. Randy can manage to score with the ladies. His beard is like a magical lure even though he's wearing the same clothes he went out in last night, so he smells a lot like a dumpster.

His last night ended a lot differently than mine. While I went home bleary-eyed with mild stomach cramps, he managed to hook up with one of the women at the BBQ. They went for a walk down to the beach and got busy in the sand. His legs and ass are covered in sand flea bites. Every few seconds he shifts around. He has to be itchy as hell. It's pretty fucking funny.

He whispers something to the chick. She giggles, pats his knee, and gets up. She's got to be a good five years older than he is or more—not that it matters. Randy likes women: short, tall, thin, curvy, blond, brunette, redhead.

"She coming back?" I ask as I watch her walk away. She's petite. Her waist is probably the same size as his right thigh.

He grins. "Maybe. I think she's gonna see if they stock condoms in that little store. She's flying first class. Her seat's beside mine."

"Did you even shower this morning?"

He scratches his balls through his shorts. "I cleaned the important parts and put on deodorant."

"You're a dirtbag."

"Whatever." He grins. "Like you can talk. I bagged it last night, so it's not like there's going to be cross-contamination."

"You're so considerate."

"You're just jealous I'm getting all the pussy you used to."

I ignore the comment and drop into the chair. It's not that I care about Randy's manwhoring ways. It's more that I've been in his shoes, and I don't want to think about how it's messing up my current attempt at a relationship. Particularly since I'm trying not to do things like that anymore. And I still feel like garbage, so I'm not in the mood.

"Still feeling crappy, huh?"

"Like Satan has taken up residence in my intestinal tract. I'll be better when we're home and I can abuse my own bathroom." I look across to where a couple of the other guys flying home today sit. Most of them have baseball caps covering their faces. It's early, and last night was rough. "They don't look any better than we do."

"Devon seems to be doing fine."

"Who?" I'm terrible with names.

"Butcher. The dude who doesn't eat meat."

"Wait, he's a butcher who doesn't eat meat?"

"No, dipshit. His last name is Butcher. He's a priest or something."

"Oooh. You're talking about The Minister." I nickname people. It's the only way I can remember them. I check him out. He is the only one in our group who doesn't look like the walking dead. "I guess he passed on the mystery meat."

"I ate the meat, and I'm fine." Randy pats his stomach. "He's all holy and stuff, so I think the only booze he can drink is wine."

"I don't think that's true." I'm almost positive I've seen Devon pounding beers a couple of times.

"I don't know. Maybe I'm talking out of my ass. Seems logical, though. They're supposed to be pure and stuff, right?"

I roll my eyes. "Dude. How much torture do you think one man can stand? He already has to feel guilty about whacking off. He'll never, ever get to put his dick in anything warm and wet and soft unless he buys something from one of those porn stores. The only good thing left is getting shitfaced."

"The thought of having to resort to something like that makes my hangover feel like it's not so bad."

I nod in agreement. "I hear orgasms help get rid of headaches. When your friend comes back from buying condoms, you can test that theory."

"I'm waiting until we're on the plane."

"I plan to destroy that bathroom like all the others I've been in today, so you might want to reconsider that option."

"I'll get there before you have a chance to annihilate it."

"Pfft. Good luck with that." I've mile-highed before. It's not as awesome as people make it out to be.

I close my eyes and lean my head against the back of the hard metal chair. I need to schedule a massage. My back is all knots. My massage therapist is going to be pissed at me for letting it get so bad. I pay her good money to manage my body, though. Plus I have a trainer who will force me to do yoga and a bunch of other non-manly-yet-super-effective training until I'm back in order.

43

Maybe Sunny'll want to give me a massage when I see her. Better yet, maybe it'll have one of those happy endings I've been hoping for.

I hunt for my phone in my backpack. I find it under an exploded power gel pack. It's covered in the sticky goo.

"Jerking it to pictures of the girlfriend again?" Randy asks. There's almost zero intonation, so it's not as funny as it could have been. Also, it would be true if Sunny was willing to send me some good pics, but I haven't asked since we're not in a place where it's kosher.

"She sent me a video message last night," I lie.

I don't know why I'm bothering to check my phone in the first place. It's totally dead. There aren't a whole lot of places in this airport to charge it, and I'm not all that interested in sitting on the floor by the one outlet across the room to make it happen. The plane will have a port. I can do it then.

I use the sleeve of Randy's shirt to clean the screen.

"What the fuck, Butterson? Did you just wipe your splooge on me?" He practically jumps out of his seat. He must stand too fast, because he stumbles and grabs his head, almost careening into a woman walking by.

He grabs her by the waist and apologizes. She looks terrified, and also possibly interested. I toss the mostly empty packet of power gel on his seat and root around for a Wet-Nap in my pack. I find one at the bottom of the bag, under the now slightly soggy kid art. Tearing it open, I clean my phone. This is when emergency bathroom run number one happens.

I'm out of my seat, clenching my ass cheeks, and gunning for the bathroom just as Randy sits on the half-empty gel pack. I'm sad I don't get to see his reaction, but I can hear him yelling, so that's something.

Karma gets me for the gel pack. Our flight ends up being delayed thanks to a three-hour rain storm. I make five more trips to the bathroom before we board the plane; two are false alarms, but the other ones are genuine emergencies. I even push someone out of the way to get to a stall. I apologize while groaning through the first wave of hell. On the positive side, the stomach cramps seem to have slowed by the time I take my seat in first class. I pull my hat down so the brim covers my eyes, stretch out my legs, and relax while the rest of plane boards.

"Sir."

A tap on my shoulder forces my eyes open. It's a real task. All I want is to sleep until we get back to the States where chicken wings come from chickens. I blink and focus on the brunette standing to my right in the blue uniform.

She's smiling the standard flight attendant smile. "All bags need to be stored in the overhead compartment for takeoff."

I'm hugging my backpack. At some point I must have started using it as a pillow. "Oh. Right."

"Do you need anything before I put it away for you?" she asks. Her eyes drop to the bag. I want to keep the Imodium with me since I've been chugging it like beer at a frat party.

"Yeah. Hold on." I open the pack, find my phone, passport, and anti-shit serum, then zip it up and pass it over.

Once she puts it away, she hands me one of those inflatable neck horseshoes. "If you need anything else during the flight, just let me know. I'd be happy to serve you."

It would be a normal thing for a flight attendant to say, except she ends it with a wink that makes it seem like she's offering more than the usual services. It wouldn't be the first time.

Takeoff is fine, apart from more stomach gurgling. Randy is in the aisle across from me, one seat back, still flirting with the woman from the lounge. If he's honestly planning to mile-high it today, he should hit the bathroom and wash off his light saber. As slutty as I've been over the years, I've never done anything that gross. Not that I can remember, anyway.

I'm reformed now. I have a girlfriend. Okay. Sunny hasn't quite agreed to be my girlfriend, but we're dating, and I'm not seeing any of the bunnies on my contact list. I'm not even answering their calls or replying to their Facebook messages, or tweets, or Instagram comments.

Getting Sunny to believe I'm only into her is more of a challenge than I expected. Relationships are way more difficult than I remember them being in high school.

During my first season in the NHL, I tried the girlfriend thing. It was long distance. I lived in Miami with the team I'd been drafted to, and she was at college in South Carolina. It didn't seem that far. I had all this money, and I hadn't learned how to manage it yet. I figured I could fly her out whenever I wanted.

It didn't turn out to be quite so easy. She met some guy in her program and broke it off with me at Christmas. After that, I decided it would be better not to get serious. There were plenty of girls who were cool with it just being about orgasms and no emotions. And I was good with that, until I met Sunny.

Since we met, we've been talking on a regular basis. I've even flown out a few times to see her. The situation is a little more complicated because of Waters.

This trip to Haiti didn't happen at the best time. Things were already a little rough with Sunny before I left. I wanted her to come with me, but she already had plans to attend some conference on karma or chi or something like that. Sunny's really into chi.

Anyway, I got a little clingy—meaning I Facebook-stalked all the posts on her wall and maybe sort of kind of threatened to kick some guy's ass for saying she looked great. I apologized, but I'm not a hundred percent positive I'm totally forgiven. Then I took a call from a bunny while Sunny was sitting right beside me.

After ten days of no contact, apart from last night's phone call, I'm thinking I need to start stepping up my game.

As an NHL player, I can get pussy whenever I want. I'm not being an egotistical jerk. I'm just stating facts. I've been cashing in on this for the past several years, so I know. After a while it starts to get a little…I don't know what the word is. Lonely, maybe? Boring? Hot sex isn't quite as hot when it's followed by selfies of me and the bunny in bed with captions like "I SCORED with Butterson!" Trophy, smiley face, celebration horn emotions included.

So I'm giving this relationship thing with Sunny one more serious shot. It's been five years since I made this kind of effort, but I figure she's worth it. If there isn't any real progress when I see her this next time, I'll consider backing off.

I want to charge my phone so I can do something useful, but unfortunately we're on one of the few planes that still hasn't been outfitted with wifi. Even if I can't check my emails and calendar, I'd at least like my phone to work when I get home, but I think the cable is in my bag in the overhead compartment. We're getting ready for takeoff, so I have to wait until we're in the air now.

A light tap on my arm draws my attention away from my dead phone. For the first time, I notice the woman beside me. Her smile is blindingly white. "I don't mean to bother you…"

I don't know why people say things like that. She obviously does mean to bother me, otherwise she wouldn't have tapped me on the arm in the first place.

"It's cool." I'll be surprised if she recognizes me with all the facial hair. Her hand is still on my arm. I glance down, the contact is unexpected and kinda uncomfortable, considering I don't even know her. She's stroking my arm hair, which is getting out of control again. I need to tame that—along with everything else—as soon as I get home and before I head to Guelph. "Do you need to get something?" I point to the overhead compartments and the seatbelt sign. "I don't think we can get up yet."

"No. No. I just. Well, God, I'm so sorry, but—"Her face turns a bright shade of red. Oh, shit. She's going to proposition me. As if to prove me right, she stops stroking my arm hair and gestures to my lap. Leaning closer, she whispers, "You have a tear in your pants."

I check out the damage. "Shitballs."

I've been living out of a bag for ten days. I haven't had access to hot, running water or decent laundry facilities. My sweats were the only semi-clean thing left, and only because I slept in them most of the trip. There's a good reason why these are my sleeping pants. The sizable hole in the crotch leaves a lot of room for exposure. Sometimes I wear these at home and fondle my balls while I watch TV. Two days ago I ran out of underwear. It's not boxers or tighty whities I'm showing her. It's my ungroomed ball sac. She might have gotten an eyeful of head as well, but I'm not sure.

I quickly rearrange my sweats. "Sorry about that. I didn't mean to flash you."

She gives my knee a squeeze and winks. "I don't think I've seen anything that exciting since before my second marriage, so there's really no need to be sorry."

This is going to be a seriously long flight.

CHAPTER THREE

THIS ISN'T THE MILE HIGH CLUB

Showing off my nuts seems to open the gate for conversation. My new friend, I'm calling her the Nut Peeper—she told me her name, but I can't remember it—chatters away, complaining about the subpar service at her five star resort.

"Where did you stay? Did you have good service?"

"I didn't stay at a resort." I wish I had my headphones and charger. The stupid seatbelt sign is still on, though, so I have to wait. Besides, if I get up I'll look like a jerk.

"Oh? Did you stay at a bed and breakfast? That's risky. You never know what kind of place it's going to be. I've heard all sorts of horror stories."

"Yeah?" I don't ask questions, but she must assume I want to know all about it, because she keeps talking.

"I had a friend who stayed in a five star B&B, and they didn't even serve breakfast! That should be standard. I can't imagine going somewhere for vacation where I had to prepare my own meals. Not unless it was a timeshare, and who wants to do that?"

In my peripheral vision I see her hand creeping along the armrest, like a fleshy spider. I'd like to squish it.

"Maybe people with food allergies?" I stupidly suggest, which gives her the green light to tell me her entire life story.

"My best girlfriend's allergic to gluten. I don't know if I believe her, though. I think she wants to be skinny, and she thinks if she can't eat bread then she can't get fat. I don't eat bread because I don't want cellulite. I only eat meat and vegetables, and I haven't gained weight in over two years. Except sometimes during the holidays, because I love rum and eggnog. But once I go back on my meat diet—poof!" She makes the accompanying hand gestures. "It's all gone again. You must be able to eat anything you want." She gives my bicep a squeeze. "Wow. You're in incredible shape. Do you do the P90X workout? What did you say you do for a living?"

The plane starts rolling, and a flight attendant appears to give us the usual safety speech. I'd much rather listen to her talk about inflating my seat if we happen to crash into a body of water than the chick beside me bitch about stupid things like eating a meat diet. In another life—maybe three months ago—I might have suggested she come to the bathroom with me so she could suck on my meat stick, but I've given that up. Kinda like people give up things for Lent—like chocolate, or swearing. Only this has been longer than forty days, and I don't have a definite end date.

Nut Peeper fidgets with her purse and produces a small prescription bottle. "I get nervous when I fly." She struggles with the cap, and suddenly I feel bad, partly because I'd considered shutting her up with my dick in her mouth, but also because her word vomit might have less to do with her being annoying and more to do with her stress level.

"Need some help?"

"Would you? Sometimes these caps are so hard to get off."

I try to read the label as I twist the tiny cap, but the word is really long, one of those "blahblah-a-blahblah-pam" jobs. I don't take medication unless I'm severely injured. I've seen enough players develop issues with painkillers, and I never want to go that way. I tend to stick to the basics like Tylenol or Advil if I'm hurting. It's only when the game's at risk and I need to get back out there and play that I'll let the team doc give me a shot of something stronger.

I pop the cap and pass it back.

"Thanks. Want one?" She asks like she's offering candy.

"I'm good."

"I might fall asleep. If I lean on you, just push me to the other side."

"Sure thing."

I don't know how many she takes, but ten minutes later she's sawing logs and trying to snuggle with my bicep. I get the flight attendant to bring blankets and an extra pillow, and then I rearrange her so she's no longer using me as her personal bed.

I don't need medication to put me to sleep. I'm exhausted, and my body hates me, so I pass out a few minutes later. I'm not sure how long I'm out for, but I'm jolted awake by a tickling feeling on my beard. I rub it and give it a scratch, but there doesn't seem to be anything in there apart from some grit and leaves and possibly leftovers from meals that didn't get washed out thanks to the limited water supply and quick, semi-cool showers.

Nut Peeper is up and flipping through a magazine. Her head bobs a couple of times, as if she's fighting to stay awake. The guy across the aisle is catching flies with his mouth. Randy and his seat friend are snuggled under a communal blanket in the row behind him.

I settle back in my chair and close my eyes. After a few minutes, it becomes clear I'm not going to fall back asleep, so I root around for my phone. The seatbelt sign is off, so I grab my bag and dig through it. I find my headphones, but not my charger. I pull everything out of the bag, including all the kid arts and crafts, but I've got nothing. I can't listen to music, and I don't even know how long I've been on the plane. I can't play mindless games on my phone to pass the time. I'll give Randy ten more minutes before I bother him for his charger. He doesn't need it since he's occupied.

Somewhere in my bag is a paper calendar. I find it at the bottom of the bag. It's soggy from the gel pack incident earlier, and the ink has bled so the words are impossible to read. There will be another paper copy at home and also one in my email, but I have to wait to check all of that. Amber's awesome at leaving plenty of reminders since I mix up dates and times a lot.

I'm a little worried about what the next couple of weeks are going to look like with her off the grid. She's going on some portaging trip in the middle of nowhere. She says she'll have her phone with her, but I can't be sure she'll have reception the whole time. Plus, she needs a break from my shit.

I shove my earbuds in and pretend to listen to music so Nut Peeper will leave me alone. I've just closed my eyes to settle in when the stomach cramps hit me again.

I don't waste any time. Unbuckling my seatbelt, I head for the bathroom, but the occupied sign taunts me with its red, annoying glare. I hope I don't shit my pants. I look around first class, checking to see who's missing from their seats. I don't see Randy, or his friend. Goddamn him. He has to be in the bathroom, boning that chick.

I move in close to the door to check if I can hear any noise inside. Oh, he's definitely fucking her. I can hear high-pitched moans. I rattle the door, hoping it's going to make them hurry the fuck up, but all I get are more moans. They're muffled this time.

"Randy, you asshole, I'm going to shit my damn pants," I whisper-yell.

I doubt he can hear me, but I knock again. It's another minute before the door finally opens and the chick steps out. Her face is flushed, her lipstick is smeared all over her face, and her hair is a mess. Her clothes are in similar shape. I don't think she has a bra on anymore. Her boobs must be fake, because her nipples are pointing right at me.

I'm standing in her way, so she can't leave the bathroom unless I take a step back.

She pats her hair and giggles as she weaves down the aisle. I can't decide if it's because she's drunk on the fumes in the washroom or because she's freshly fucked and it's hard to walk.

Randy's still zipping up his pants as he leaves the bathroom.

"I left you a present."

He pats me on the shoulder and struts down the aisle. I'm practically holding my ass as I launch myself into the bathroom. There's pee all over the seat. Randy's or someone else's I don't know, but his gift is a spent, splooge-filled condom in the sink. Fucking asshole.

I grab a handful of toilet paper and rush to clean off the seat because this has gone from a level-one to a level-five emergency. I dry heave over the strong smell and the feel of pee soaking through the paper. I'm going to eat asparagus and piss in Randy's hockey bag the first chance I get.

My stomach cramps again; I'm out of time. I drop my drawers, grateful for the lack of underwear and sit my ass down. I don't even care that the seat is still slightly damp. There's no time for anything but relief as the first wave hits me. I lean my head against the tiny metal sink. I don't care about the germs or the stink or how badly I need a shower and maybe some medicated pads to soothe my ass. I feel like the new guy in prison right now.

I'm not sure how long I spend in the bathroom, but I triple flush. At some point there's a knock on the door and someone asks if I'm okay. I might be groaning. I have the cold sweats again. I just want it to be over. I want my own bathroom and my bed. I want my girlfriend. Well, maybe not. I don't want Sunny to see me in this state, but if we'd been dating longer, and I had the flu instead of this, it'd be nice to have someone comfort me.

Since it was just me and my dad growing up, whenever I got sick he'd make me instant chicken noodle soup. I could go for a cup of that right about now, even if it might come back up, or out, depending.

Eventually the cramps pass, and it feels safe to leave the bathroom. I can't hijack it for the whole flight. Plus, the smell in here is making my stomach turn in a different way.

I pry myself off the seat and wash my arms up to my elbows in the sink made for dwarves or elves, or whatever small creatures can use these stupid things effectively without getting water everywhere. I check my pockets to make sure I haven't lost anything, palming my phone in the process. Randy's damn well gonna give me his charger for making me deal with pee all over the seat.

I steady myself and open the door, aware I'm about to do the gastrointestinal version of the walk of shame. I've been in here longer than it takes most people to join the Mile High Club.

At the same time as I try to leave the bathroom, the plane jerks with turbulence. The woman standing outside the door, who incidentally happens to be Nut Peeper, is thrown inside with me. Most of the time I have excellent balance. Today I don't. She falls into me, grabbing my shirt as I stumble back.

In the melee, I lose my grip on my phone, along with my footing. The phone hits something metal with a concerning clang. I say a prayer to the phone-preservation gods that it doesn't break, as every last important thing in my life is on that phone.

The door automatically shut me and Nut Peeper in together when she fell on me. These bathrooms are barely big enough for me, never mind adding another body, so maneuvering around in the cramped space is even more difficult. Plus, I'm a little claustrophobic, which is unfortunate since I'm big and it makes most spaces feel small.

"Oh my God. I'm so sorry!" She flails around. It's the opposite of helpful. I have to brace myself on something to stop her from ending up with her face in my crotch. I put my hand down, and of course it ends up in wet spot. I don't even want to know if it's pee.

"It smells awful in here!" She tries to clamp a hand over her mouth and nose, but it manages to get caught in my shirt. All she ends up doing is mashing her face into my diaphragm and knocking us off balance again.

"I ate something bad last night," I say, as if an explanation is necessary for why it smells like a manure field and a dead skunk combined with whatever crap they put in here to help mask the smell of people's bodily functions.

I'm going to need to Purell my entire body when this episode is over.

Using the surface I'm braced against for resistance, I wrap my free arm around her waist to stop the flailing and manage to get us into an upright position. She's still fisting my shirt even though there's no reason anymore. I grab both of her arms, not caring that the likely-pee on my hand is getting all over her. If it wasn't for Nut Peeper, I wouldn't have it on my hand in the first place.

"Stop moving!" I order.

She freezes.

"I dropped my phone. I need to find it before one of us steps on it."

"Oh, no!"

"Oh, yeah." I let go of her, confident she won't move, and scan the floor. It's a tiny space, but I can't see the device anywhere. Checking over my shoulder, I spot it. It's in the worst place possible: sitting in the goddamn toilet. It's got one of those protective cases, but I doubt it safeguards against chemically treated toilet water and poop particles.

"Shitsicles."

"What's wrong?" She grabs my arm again. I'm starting to think she's doing it on purpose.

"It's in the toilet."

"Oh. Ew. That's so gross. You shouldn't use your phone in public bathrooms."

There's no response I can give that isn't going to make me sound like an asshole. I might have a right to be one, but I don't get to act like one unless I'm on the ice. Otherwise, it ends up in the media, all twisted around.

I have no other option but to stick my hand in there and get it. I maneuver to face the bowl of doom. Before I shove my hand in, I try to convince myself it's the same as sticking my finger in an ass—like during foreplay. It doesn't work, though, I'm still on the verge of gagging. I grab some of the rough, single-ply toilet paper to minimize contact. Whatever's been in that toilet, it can't be worse than some of the bunnies I've been with.

Except I can wrap my dick and give it a wash when the dirty is over. Not quite so easy in this case.

An announcement over the PA system warns us that we need to get back to our seats. A tiny bump follows, as if to drive the point home. Nut Peeper must have the worst balance in the world. She slams into me from behind, and I bang my head on the wall. I throw out my hand to stop from face planting into the bowl. I'm about six inches away from my poor phone, lying in the toilet bowl. It better still work, or I'm screwed.

Nut Peeper is making full-body contact. "Are you okay? I don't know what's wrong with me. I'm so sorry. I thought it was a good opportunity to use the bathroom with you out of your seat. You're so big, and I wouldn't have been able to get around you if you fell asleep again. I have a tiny bladder. I should probably have surgery."

I shake her off and reach for my phone just as the sound of suction fills the tiny room. The little hole in the toilet opens, threatening to claim my phone.

"No!" I snatch it up before it can disappear forever.

"I'm so sorry! I didn't mean to hit the button!" She's latched onto me again, like a damn leech, peering over my shoulder.

"My phone almost got sucked down the toilet!"

There's a knock at the door. "Sir? We're experiencing turbulence. You must return to your seat immediately."

"I'll be right out!" I spin around, almost elbowing the chick in the neck, as I turn on the tap. I don't know what I'm thinking as I hold my phone under the spray, other than I need to clean it off and that I'll have to forever use speaker phone until I get a new one. Which I'll be doing tomorrow.

"Won't that ruin the phone?" asks Nut Peeper.

"Shit. Goddamn it!" I turn off the water and nab a handful of paper towels. I'd use my shirt, but it's just as disgusting as the phone.

"You probably shouldn't have done that."

"Probably not, but it was covered in intestinal juice."

"Ew. That's gross."

"It's your damn fault. Why are you even still in here?"

"Because of the turbulence, remember?" She's looking at me like I'm crazy, when it's clear she's the one a few bricks short of a load.

The flight attendant knocks on the door again, more insistently this time. "Sir? Only *one* person is allowed in the bathroom at a time. You need to come out now."

I throw up my hands. "Great. Now we're in trouble. Could this day get any goddamn worse?" I reach around Nut Peeper and throw open the door. The flight attendant's concern changes to disgust when she takes in my appearance and the woman in front of me. She looks equally disheveled, although she's not covered in blue toilet water like I am.

"It's not what it looks like." For once in my life it's true, except based on our appearances, I sound like a liar.

The flight attendant rolls her eyes. "Both of you need to return to your seats now. The seatbelt sign is on." She points to the lighted sign above the door.

Nut Peeper slinks out of the stall and wobbles down the aisle, banging into almost everyone as she goes, drawing more attention to me. People are already staring because of all the noise. Randy looks over the back of the seat and gives me a look like he disapproves of my choice. Dickhead.

"Sir, I won't tell you again." The flight attendant crosses her arms over her chest.

I gesture to the chick as she flops into her seat. "She fell into the bathroom when I was trying to leave, and then my phone fell in the toilet. My hands have been in that germ-infested water. I need to wash them. What if someone gets pink eye, or E.coli, or botulism?"

She just stares. She obviously doesn't believe me.

"Why would I lie? Honestly. Come on. The only thing I'm responsible for is polluting the toilet." She makes a TMI face, which I ignore. I don't know why I want her to believe me so badly. I guess it's just that for once I'm not being a dog, and I want some acknowledgement.

"None of this would have happened if she hadn't gotten trapped in the bathroom with me. Just ask her. I wasn't trying to mile-high it. Look at the size of me. I barely fit in one of these bathrooms. Take a whiff. It doesn't smell like sex in there."

I move to the side, and in doing this, I give her a full view of the damage. There's water all over the place. But that's not what puts a look of disgust on her face.

"Not trying to join the Club, huh?" She pulls a pen out of her pocket and lifts the spent condom out of the sink, holding it up for me to see.

"It's not mine. I swear."

Her eyes narrow, and she lowers her voice to a whisper. "I know who you are. I think what you're doing is repulsive. I hope Waters sticks you in the throat for what you're doing to his sister. You're a disgrace to hockey."

It's the most demeaning insult a person can give me. What's worse is that it's centered on a misunderstanding. But I know how it all looks, and based on my reputation, I can see why she won't believe what I have to say.

A few months ago, I probably would've gotten busy with that chick just to make the flight go by faster, but that was the old me. The new me keeps my hands to myself and keeps other people's hands off me. The second part seems to be the most difficult. I only have control over my body parts, not anyone else's.

I go to rub my face with my hand until I remember it's got pee and chemicals on it.

In my peripheral vision, I spot a crack in the curtain they pull across to separate the first class passengers from the economy class. A teenage boy in the second row holds his phone above the seat. As soon as he sees me looking he lowers the phone a few inches and makes like he's typing. I know better. After years of being caught doing things I shouldn't, it's not a surprise that someone's recording this whole stupid episode.

I point at the kid. "Stop that!"

He hits a button, and then his phone flashes a number of times. At least he's stopped filming, but the pictures aren't going to be any better since I'm pissed off.

"Aren't you going to stop him?" I ask the flight attendant. She doesn't seem to see the issue. I poke my head through the curtain like the guy in that old Stephen King movie. "If you post that I'll have my lawyers sue you for defamation of character." I pretend to take a picture of him with my phone. "I have facial recognition software. I'll be able to find out what your name is and where you live."

"Sir!"

The flight attendant tries to get around me. I'm too broad, though. I take up most of the aisle, and she definitely doesn't want to touch me.

The kid's eyes bug out, and he finally puts his phone away. I can't relax, though, because I doubt he's going to delete the video. I don't know how much he heard or what exactly he recorded, but I don't want this leaked to the media. Especially if he caught the used dome hanging off the flight attendant's pen.

I'd take refuge in the fact that it's probably a grainy video, but I'm wearing a team hat, and if enough people see it, someone will recognize me, and I'll get tagged. It'll be a shitshow. I'll have to run interference with Vi, since Alex will shit a brick and threaten to kick my ass, again. If he thinks I banged someone in a public bathroom, on a plane, he'll probably break my nose, just like I broke his earlier in the year. That was at least justifiable. The dickhead denied being with my sister on public television. And she still moved in with him.

Beyond that, I'll have to explain it to Sunny and dig myself out of a hole that doesn't exist. I really hate those chicken wings, Nut Peeper, Randy, cell phones, and social media right now. This is officially the shittiest flight I've ever been on.

I realize all the people in economy are looking at me, including the guys I went on the trip with. The plane does that shuddery thing again. I back out and pull the curtains closed.

The flight attendant braces her hand on the door. "If you don't return to your seat immediately, I'm going to have you banned from this airline."

I'm still covered in toilet water. It's all down my shirt and still all over my hands. It's probably on my ass, as well. My head hurts from more than the hit on the bathroom wall.

"Okay. I'm going. I'm just gonna wash my hands. I don't want to contaminate the plane. I pretty much landed in the toilet when that lady crashed into the bathroom on me." I reach for the bathroom door but she blocks the way.

"I can't sit through the rest of the flight smelling like this. It's not fair to the other people on the plane. Everyone'll be using their barf bags."

The flight attendant huffs, but she opens the door. She watches as I pump half the contents of the dispenser into my hands and soap my forearms up to my elbow, again. I can't tell if it's the bathroom or me that smells like pee at this point.

I move on to my face after I finish my arms. She clears her throat, an indication that I'm pushing it now. I've got three more hours on this plane, though. If I'm going to be banned from the bathroom, I want to smell less like a toilet and more like cheap airline soap.

Once I'm as clean as I'm going to get, I head down the aisle. I stop at Randy's seat. "I need your phone charger."

"Fuck that, you're not getting it."

"Why not?"

Randy gives me this look that tells me he thinks I should know. He nods in the direction of my seat where Nut Peeper is reapplying lipstick and fluffing her hair. "Not cool, man."

"Dude. I didn't—"

The flight attendant clears her throat from behind me. I shake my head, annoyed that he could think I'd do something like that, and return to my seat. I want to grab my backpack from the overhead compartment. I have a spare shirt in there, but I have a feeling the flight attendant might junk-punch me if I do.

Nut Peeper apologizes seventy-five times. I can't even pretend to listen to music because she thinks she broke my phone.

I shove the device in my pocket, close my eyes, and pretend to sleep until they turn off the seatbelt sign. I don't know how long the reprieve is going to last, so I grab my bag from the overhead bin. My spare shirt is dirty, but it doesn't smell like poop, so it's a step up. I'm not risking another trip to the bathroom so I sit down to change my shirt.

I don't hear the click of the camera, but the flash indicates Nut Peeper is taking pictures of me shirtless. I get my toilet shirt over my head. My hat pops off and ends up in the aisle where the flight attendant runs it over with her drink cart. Shoving my hands through the sleeves I pull the cleaner shirt over my abs.

"Really?" I ask as the clicking continues.

She doesn't even look embarrassed as she shrugs. "Can you blame me? I didn't realize who you were until some kid in economy got excited about you being in the bathroom. Do you think I can get your autograph?"

I don't say any of the things I want to. "I don't have a pen."

"I do!" She pulls out her purse and hands me a sparkly pink one.

"What do you want me to sign?"

"How about this?" She motions to her chest.

I keep my eyes on her face. "I can't sign that."

"Why not?"

"Because I have a girlfriend, and I want it to stay that way."

"Oh. That's too bad." She rummages around in her purse and finds a crumpled piece of paper. "Can you make it out to

Guinevere?"

Of course she has to have one of those long, difficult names. At least it's reasonable for me to ask how to spell it so I don't mess it up. She practically sits on top of me while I scribble a message and sign my name.

"Thanks, Buck! Can I get a picture, too?" She doesn't wait for my response. She snuggles in real close and snaps half a dozen selfies before I can even think to smile.

If that kid's video doesn't end up on the internet, these pictures will, or the ones of me shirtless on a plane. All I can do is hope I can talk to Sunny before they go viral, along with whatever ridiculous and inaccurate story gets posted along with them.

PUCKED OVER: THE OUTTAKES

There are three Pucked Over outtakes so far, all from Randy's POV, because, well, he's the man. I honestly fell so in love with writing this couple. The first outtake is an alternate POV of the Laundry Room scene and the second I wrote for Valentine's Day. I've also added the Valentine's Day letter Randy wrote for Lily, expressing his feelings in words, not just actions. The final outtake comes from a pivotal scene in Pucked Over, because it signified a lot of trust on Randy's part, and it really was the moment where these two truly started to recognize that this wasn't just about the hook up anymore.

THE LAUNDRY ROOM

Usually travel days bag me, but it doesn't matter that I've been on the road since dawn, or that I smell like the inside of an airplane. Lily's in Chicago. For multiple days. And this time I'm going to have more than twenty-four consecutive hours in which to get her naked.

I don't think I've ever been this fucking excited to fuck, like, ever. Plus sleepovers. And pussy prison.

"Dude, I feel like I'm on a freaking amusement park ride. Relax," Lance knocks his knee against mine.

I didn't even realize I was bouncing my leg. I tap my fingers on my knee instead, but it's not working. I'm keyed right up.

I figure once the girls get here, we only have to stay for max half an hour, then I'll make up some excuse and take Lily back to my place. And then it's a fuck free-for-all. I even bought her new panties and some fun "sleep wear," which is really just expensive scraps of lace that aren't going to stay on very long.

I pull out my phone and send her a message:

> I can't wait 4 pussy prison.

Her message back tells me they'll be here in ten minutes, so I run upstairs to one of the spare bathrooms and hunt down some mouthwash and deodorant so I don't smell like crap. When I come back down, Alex is yelling for a hand with the bags.

Which means Lily's here.

I take the stairs two at a time.

And there she is—wearing jeans and a long-sleeved shirt, face flushed, hair flipping out at the ends. I barely let her in the door before I pick her up and crush her against me. I know, without a doubt, that I'm way more invested than I should be in this girl, but I can't seem to give a fuck right now.

I'm already hard. Already thinking about how soon I can get her back to my place. And maybe not give her back.

She shrieks and giggles as I bury my face against her neck and breathe her in. She smells like she's been drinking, and her skin is warm and sweet, like it always is. I part my lips against her neck and suck, then bite my way to her ear. "I can't wait to go to pussy prison."

I don't think she even realizes that she moans, or that it's loud. I glance up to find all my friends staring at me. Lance looks like he's trying not to shit his pants. Miller and Alex both kind of look like they want to kill me right now, and Darren is amused, which is typical. But all I want is a few minutes alone with Lily.

I spin around and survey the hall heading for the closest door. As long as it has a lock on it, we're good to go.

"No way, Balls!" Miller shouts. "You and Lily aren't allowed in bathrooms together!"

I laugh and sidestep inside. It's not a bathroom; it's the laundry room. Even better—there are solid surfaces.

I try to shut the door, but Miller's leaning against it. He's a big guy, with a good thirty pounds on me, and that's when he's not bulking up. But I have something I want, and she's standing right in front of me with those luscious lips parted, looking like she wants to be devoured as much as I want to devour her.

I lean into the door, pushing hard. I still have one arm wrapped around Lily's waist, so I set her down, giving myself the advantage.

"I need a little something right here." I tap my lips.

Lily glances at the mostly closed door and at Miller's shoulder pressed against it, and she smiles, coy and sweet. She steps in close and runs her fingers through my hair. Her nails scratch my scalp and skim behind my ear. I feel like I'm an addict. Her touch is the drug I crave, and right now I'm about to get my first hit.

She rises up on her toes and brushes her mouth over mine, tongue peeking out to touch my lip.

"Seriously, Balls, can't you wait, like, five minutes?" Miller grunts.

"I'm just saying hello, and I'm looking for a little privacy to do that." I shove with my shoulder and the door slams closed, so I turn the lock, ignoring Miller's shouts. "And now we have some."

Lily winds her arms around my neck as I lift her up and set her on the closest surface, which happens to be a dryer. It's the perfect height. Lily parts her thighs for me and scoots forward, wrapping her legs around my waist. And then we start grinding on each other.

I can't get enough of tasting her, so I kiss a path up her neck, ready for her mouth.

"You're terrible," she whispers, then gasps when I grab her ass and pull her tighter against me.

"I know. We don't have to stay here long—like, fifteen minutes, and then we can go back to my place where we can play until you have to go back to Canadia."

Someone knocks on the door. It's probably Miller, but I'm right where I want to be, so I'm not inclined to stop what I'm doing. In fact, I'm wondering how hard it would be to get her naked right now, except the knocking is a little damn distracting. I try to slide a hand down the back of her jeans, but they're too tight.

"Why're you wearing pants? They're so inconvenient."

Lily laughs. It's breathy and soft, but she tightens her legs around me, and I keep on grinding. The laugh turns into a moan, and she breaks out in goosebumps.

I'm pretty much dry-fucking her. And that's when I realize,

this is just like that time in the bathroom at the exhibition game. All the signs are there: the way she's gripping my hair, the little moans that get louder with every shift of her hips, the soft whimper that turns into my name.

I slip a hand under her shirt, skimming soft, hot skin until I reach the underside of her bra. It feels like satin. Pushing the cup up, I find her nipple and brush my thumb over it, feeling the skin tighten in response.

"I seriously need you naked. It's not even funny," I groan against her mouth.

Clearly she feels the same way, because she starts rubbing on me harder, faster, and her grip on my hair tightens even more.

I break the kiss, biting back a smile at her despondent whimper. "You're gonna come aren't you?"

She nods furiously. "Uh-huh."

"I should be inside you for that."

She groans again, gripping the back of my neck like she's trying to get my mouth back.

But I want to see her come. I want to see what happens when I barely touch her, because I know later, when there aren't any clothes in the way, I get to put my mouth on her, and be inside her, and watch all those orgasms happen, because I make it so.

I pinch her nipple hard and pull her in tight. I feel her toes curling against the back of my legs. Her entire body goes still for a fraction of a second, and then she shakes hard, like she's trying to control it. But she can't, just like I can't control this thing happening with her. And if I don't get to be in control, neither does she.

Lily bites her lip, as if she's holding in the sound that comes with the sensations, but she doesn't have control of that either. It's a high-pitched moan that includes my name. Her eyes are wide, her lips parted, breath coming in sharp gasps. And the way she's looking at me, like I'm the only one who exists in her world, is the reason I want to keep her.

She's not done coming, not even close, when the door bursts

open. Her muscles are tight, and her panic is clear. "Ride it out," I whisper.

I don't take my eyes off her, though, because watching her come is my favorite thing—apart from just being in her physical presence.

"Oh, wow." That's Sunny.

"Is she—" Charlene starts.

"Oh, definitely," Violet interjects. "Check out her toes."

Lily looks embarrassed as fuck, but I can't stop smiling. I'll deal with the epic case of blue balls I'm gonna be rocking to see her lose it like that.

Just for me.

THE VALENTINE'S DAY
LETTER

Luscious Lily,

We both know I'm more of an action man than a words guy, but if there's ever a time to tell you how I feel, I'm guessing Valentine's Day is it.

So here goes . . .

When I think about you I feel . . . hard in my pants.
When I see you I feel . . . like I need to get you naked pretty much immediately, which isn't always reasonable, especially when we're out in public or we have company.
When you're naked I feel . . . like I can't get my hands on you fast enough.
When I make you come I feel . . . like the king of your universe.
When I'm away from you I feel . . . like I'm missing the most important part of me.
When I'm with you I feel . . . like the world could be ending and it wouldn't matter, because I have you.

You're the best thing in my life.

Happy Valentine's Day

Yours, moody dick and all ;)

Raucous Randy

THE VALENTINE'S DAY OUTTAKE

Miller taps his fingers on the steering wheel as another pop song comes on the radio. I arch a brow at his questionable music choice, but he's focused on the road. Actually, he's looking at a billboard. I follow his gaze. It's an advertisement for perfume boasting a half-naked chick in lingerie.

"Shit. Valentine's Day is next week."

He's all smirky. "I've already taken care of Sunny's present."

"What'd you get her?"

"Something special." His grin widens.

"Putting a bow on your dick doesn't actually count. You know that, right?"

"I leave dick dressup to Waters," he mutters, flipping me the bird.

"Whoa, what?"

"Nothing. Never mind." He stares straight ahead.

"You can't say something like that and not tell me what the hell that means. Dick dressup?" Waters is one weird guy. "How would you even know what the hell Waters does with his dick?"

"Violet's my sister, remember? And she likes to share. A lot."

Most of the time Violet's excessive sharing is funny. Sometimes it's a little overboard. I'd never tell my sister the things Violet tells Miller. "So what's the most recent accidental information dump?"

He gives me a shifty side-eye. "You can't tell anyone. Not even Lily."

71

"This is gonna be good."

"I'm serious, Balls, you can't say anything."

I hold my fingers up, like I'm giving him the Boy Scouts salute, when really I'm giving him the shocker.

"Forget it. I'm not telling you. Violet was drunk. She probably didn't mean to say anything."

"Come on, bro. Seriously. I'll keep my mouth shut." I stop smiling and put my hand over my heart. "What weirdness do those two get up to in the bedroom?"

Miller grips the steering wheel and releases a few times. "You won't tell Lily?"

"I swear on my nearly severed dick."

His eyes widen and he nods, releasing a breath. Whatever it is, it must be good.

"Remember the Play-Doh dick sculpture from the cottage?"

"Huh?" I frown and then smirk remembering what happened with Lily that weekend. Not all of it was good at the time, but now we're together, and she's living in Chicago. We have a lot of sleepovers. She pretty much stays with me all the time when I'm not away for games.

"The one on the dining room table that the girls took pictures of," Miller prompts.

"Oh, yeah. You mean the one with the superhero cape?"

"Yeah. Apparently she's actually done that."

"Hold up." I raise a hand, trying to understand what he's telling me. "So she does what? Dresses up Waters' dick? And he lets her?"

"I don't think he lets her. I mean, from the story she told me, he was asleep when she pulled that on him, but apparently she made some sort of Christmas thing. I don't even know." He's backpedaling now. "Anyway, she mentioned she had some sort of plan for Valentine's Day."

"Those two are seriously weird."

Miller nods.

"Yeah, well, I'm not dressing up my dick for Valentine's Day and presenting it to Lily like it's some kind of gift."

"Hard to do when she already owns it, Balls."

"Like you're any better. Sunny carries your fuzzy balls around in her back pocket."

He shrugs like it doesn't matter that he's totally whipped. And honestly, I don't mean anything I'm saying. Lily and I haven't been together all that long, but during the very short span of time when we "broke up," I learned I didn't want to be without her.

"What do you think I should get Lily?" I ask. I've never done the Valentine's Day gift thing before. In the past it would have given the girl the wrong idea about what was going on. But I don't have to worry about that since Lily's my girlfriend. What I do need to worry about is getting her a decent gift.

"What does she like? Other than sex and your beard."

"Skating, ketchup chips, bacon," I say.

"Seriously, Balls?"

"I don't know. Can't I just buy her chocolate and flowers? I bet that asshole ex of hers didn't even do that."

"Probably not and yeah, I guess you could, but it's kind of a copout."

"So you're not getting Sunny flowers or chocolate?"

"She's vegan, so regular chocolate is out, and Sunny's house is already filled with plants. She doesn't need any more."

He has a point. There's a lot of live, green things in that house. I can't even keep the one spider plant Lily brought to my place alive. "What about jewelry?"

"Does she like jewelry?"

Lily wears tiny hoop earrings that she never takes out, and she has a total of two necklaces.

"Maybe she just doesn't have anything she likes?" I muse. Or it's always been too frivolous of an expense. Lily's never had an excess supply of money, so she's had to be careful with it. Sometimes it makes it difficult for her to accept gifts.

"Maybe," Miller agrees.

"I could ask her."

"Doesn't that kind of defeat the purpose? It should be a surprise."

"Right. Yeah." Seems like Valentine's Day is a lot more complicated than I anticipated.

-6-

I spend the next couple of days trying to decide what I want to do. Lily's like a damn fortress for information, though, and I can't get anything out of her. I try to casually bring it up while we're watching TV the night before I have two away games. We're in our usual position, with Lily tucked into the corner of the couch, her legs thrown over my lap. She's wearing pajama shorts and a long-sleeved shirt. There's no bra under the shirt. I can see her nipples poking through it.

She's eating maple-bacon popcorn. It's her new obsession. She doesn't even bother with a bowl, just eats it right out of the bag.

"Valentine's Day is coming up," I say.

She shoves a handful of popcorn in her mouth and makes an affirmative noise.

"We should go out to dinner."

She swallows the popcorn and glances at me. "If you want."

"Well, yeah, I mean, it's, like, a special day, right?"

She shrugs. "I guess."

I know exactly what that means. The ex asshole definitely didn't do anything nice for her for Valentine's Day. Now I really wish I would've kicked his ass at Waters' cottage when I had the chance.

I'm about to go on a fishing expedition using my classic Ballistic charm. Of all the traits I inherited from my dickhead dad, my ability to smooth talk is one I don't mind. It gets me what I want a lot of the time. I run a hand up her bare shin to her knee and knead the spot there. She sighs and slides down a little lower. I adjust with her movement so my hand doesn't go any higher, like I'm sure she wants it to.

"You don't want to do anything for Valentine's Day?"

She stops shoveling popcorn into her mouth and sets the bag down. She regards me carefully.

"You think you're so charming, don't you?"

I grin. "Uh-huh."

Lily rolls her eyes. "How many women have fallen for that look?"

"Only one who matters." I walk my fingers a little higher.

"Right answer."

I don't get any further with the Valentine's Day conversation. I get distracted when she takes her shirt off and we start making out. We end up having sex on the couch, then on the floor, then in bed. Additional information is unnecessary anyway. Her reaction, or lack thereof, tells me more than words could.

Lily needs to be treated like the delicate flower she sometimes is. And I'm going to make that happen.

Five days before Valentine's Day, and just before I get on the plane, I call Lily's favorite restaurant. She's spent most of her life not having enough, or sacrificing herself for the sake of other people, so I want to give her the luxuries she's never been able to afford.

I discover that Valentine's Day is a kind of a big damn deal, especially when it falls on a weekend, so getting a table ends up being a huge fucking hassle. I have contacts, though, so I manage to work it out. It'll be a late dinner, but that's not necessarily a bad thing.

I secure us an excellent table and order flowers—lilies, of course—that will be delivered first thing in the morning to my place, since she stays with me when I'm home. A box of chocolates is scheduled to arrive around lunch time, because

Lily loves chocolate almost as much as she loves sex. Then I shop online for jewelry because I don't have time to go to an actual store. I also call Sunny to get the name of the spa they go to. I confer with Miller, and we set up appointments for both of them.

There's a fine line with extravagance where Lily's concerned. If something's too expensive, she gets antsy about it. I'm learning where her lines are, and slowly erasing them. She's going to have to deal with excess at some point, because I want to give her everything.

Lily may be independent, but she likes pretty things, and while she might not say it outright, I see how she gets when I buy her stuff. I'm sly about it. I don't shower her with gifts. She doesn't like that. Instead I play it off like I just saw something and liked it and thought she should have it. Or I'll hang it up with the things that have found a home in my closet or my dresser like it's been there the whole time.

Her eyes light up every time I bring her a present, or she finds something new hanging in the closet. And I like it. I like taking care of her like that. But I would never say that out loud to her face. I know better.

The only thing I tell Lily about Valentine's Day is that we have dinner plans. Everything else is going to be a surprise. Thankfully I have the day off and no practice or workout because we flew in late last night.

Usually after a few days away, Lily and I have a lot of sex, but I want to hold off until tomorrow for that, so we only go a couple of rounds before bed. I don't wake her up in the middle of the night like I normally would. Then I get up early and make her breakfast.

Okay, I don't exactly make breakfast on my own, but I pour the batter into the waffle iron and hull the strawberries, so it counts in my mind.

I get everything ready, put it on a tray, and bring it to the bedroom. She's migrated to my side of the bed and curled herself around my pillow. Her hair's all fucked up in the back from the sex last night.

I stroke her cheek. "Luscious Lily, time to get up."

She makes a little noise and burrows deeper into my pillow. She's totally awake. I get up on the bed, straddle her, and rub my nose and beard against her cheek. I feel her grin as she squirms to get away.

"I'm sleeping," she mumbles.

"I made you breakfast in bed."

She stops squirming and rolls over on her back. The covers fall away from her chest, exposing her little pink nipples. I resist the urge to kiss them. For now.

She blinks. "Really?"

"Uh-huh." I gesture to the tray on the dresser.

"You didn't have to do that." Her smile tells me I did the right thing.

"I know. I wanted to. Hungry?"

She nods, so I bring the tray over, and we eat until we're full and her eyes get heavy like she's ready for a nap.

After I take the leftovers to the kitchen, I get the present I ordered online from its hiding place. It came pre-wrapped. I keep it behind my back and climb into bed with her, ready for a lazy day of indulgence, lots of sex, and possibly a nap, if required. "I have something for you."

Her eyes light up. "You do?"

"Uh-huh."

"What is it?"

I hold out my hand. The box fits in my palm. "Open it and find out."

Lily blinks and looks at the box, then at me, then at the box. Her eyes are wide. "Randy."

"It's just something small." Literally, it's tiny. But that

77

doesn't mean it wasn't expensive.

Since she hasn't taken the box from me, I set it on her lap and wait. I'm nervous. Maybe she won't like it. Maybe I guessed wrong.

Her hands are a little shaky as she pulls the red ribbon and the bow unfurls. I have to clasp mine together so I don't start biting my thumbnail, which is a leftover nervous habit from when I was a kid and my parents used to fight.

Lily takes the long satin ribbon and wraps it around her neck. "Wanna tie that back up for me?"

I'm instantly hard. A few weeks ago Lily surprised me after an away game by answering my door with nothing but a ribbon tied around her throat. It was awesome, though Lance was with me, which was not awesome. But he's smart enough not to have commented on it, ever.

Maybe it was the ribbon, or my irrational, but somewhat justified anger over Lance seeing her naked, or coming home to her after a long stretch away, or the combination of all three, but I've been fantasizing about that damn scenario a lot since then. I skim the column of her throat and tie it nice and loose.

"You better hurry up and open that, or you're not gonna get to see what's inside for at least another hour."

She bites her lip and grins, but lifts the lid. "Oh, wow."

"Is it too cheesy? It's too cheesy." I'm second-guessing my choice based on her expression.

She shakes her head. "They're not cheesy. They're beautiful." She lifts the tiny skate-shaped earrings out of the box. One's a figure skate, one's a hockey skate—mismatched on purpose.

"They're supposed to be charms, and I know they're different, but I kind of like that it's you and me and they're different, but if you'd rather they be the same…"

"They're perfect."

"Or if you'd rather wear them as a necklace, we can put them on a chain—"

"Randy?"

I stop. "Yeah?"

"I love them."

"Yeah?" I pull her into my lap. She's naked; I'm in boxers. It won't take much to make us match. "Guess what I love?"

Her eyes are soft and warm. "What do you love, Randy?"

I trace the edge of the ribbon around her throat, watching goosebumps rise along her skin. The words I've felt but haven't spoken hang heavy in the space between us. "You. I love you."

There's no surprise. Just acceptance and reciprocation. "Just like I love you," she whispers.

And then I show her how much, because words are only as deep as the actions we take to make them meaningful.

PUCKED OVER OUTTAKE

THE FUCKING CONE

Randy

I'm not even a little bit on board with this scheme Violet has cooked up. What's worse is that everyone else, apart from Miller, seems fine with it. Lily just got here, and already people are monopolizing my time with her.

My initial plan was to have one beer and then make up some lame excuse so I could hijack Lily and take her back to my place. Then we could have as much sex as we wanted without any interference or interruptions for as long as she's here.

But clearly my night is not going according to plan, because Lily is now back at Waters' house watching some dumb chick movie with the girls, and I'm sitting in Waters' SUV, surrounded by the same guys I've been with for the past week. As a result, I'm in a shit mood.

Lance gets in beside me. "We should go to Mahoney's to watch the game, right, Balls?"

"Whatever," I grumble. Mahoney's will be full of bunnies I'm not interested in dealing with.

Miller gets in on the other side, sandwiching me between them. Miller's a tank and so is Lance, so I'm crammed in like a damn sardine. Or maybe my crappy mood doesn't allow for much in the way of tolerance. The only physical contact I want right now is Lily all over me.

My balls are seriously blue—like, a raging, horrible ache that isn't going to go away until my dick is inside Lily. Thinking about being inside Lily—all hot and tight and wet—makes the ache worse. I shift around, trying to create some room for my damn balls, which feel like they're the size of grapefruits, even though I know they're not.

"Wanna get out of my lap?" I snap at Miller.

He gives me the raised eyebrow. "Don't get pissy with me."

"Guess yer seven minutes in heaven wasn't all that awesome, yeah, Balls?" Lance says.

"It woulda been fine if I was now on my way back to my place with Lily instead of here with a bunch of sausage."

"I didn't realize this thing with you and Lily was getting serious." Alex glances at me in the rear-view mirror.

"It's not."

Westinghouse looks over his shoulder from the passenger seat. "You sure about that?"

"We're just—"

"—having fun," Miller and Lance say at the same time.

Westinghouse snorts, and Lance and Miller fist-bump each other behind my head.

"You guys are a bunch of assholes."

"Wanna check the glove compartment for some tampons? Looks like Balls has his period," Lance says.

"Fuck you," I shoot back.

"Lily's not really a casual kind of girl. She was in a serious relationship for a long time and just got out of it pretty recently," Alex says.

"Yeah, I know that. Which is why this isn't serious. I'm, like, the pre-next-boyfriend training wheels or whatever you want to call it."

"Just watch yourself, Balls. She's a sweet girl, and her ex was a dick. She hasn't really done a lot of playing the field." Alex punctuates this with a pointed look.

It's as clear a warning as I'm going to get. I've been waiting for it, to be honest. Miller's said the same thing pretty much constantly since Lily and I started hooking up.

Miller gives me a not-so-subtle elbow to the ribs, his own version of I-told-you-so. I don't say anything for the rest of the ride to the bar. I'm not in the mood to catch any more shit.

Waters and Westinghouse must come here a lot, because as soon as we walk in, one of the hostesses welcomes us, then flits away to get a table ready. She seems flustered by our unexpected arrival. She must apologize six times for not having his usual table available. Alex reassures her it's not a big deal, and that we didn't expect to be out tonight. He must come here with Violet because she asks about her, too.

I could handle this a lot better if Lily were here rather than back at Waters' place. Without me.

I wait until everyone else is seated before I take my spot at the end of the table. I immediately start in with the texts to Lily.

"Dude, put your phone away. You're gonna see her in a few hours. She'll be here all week," Miller mutters.

"Easy for you to say. Sunny's moving here in a month. All I have is a week, and then who fucking knows when I'll see Lily again."

With Sunny moving to Chicago, it might very well mean I'll see more of Lily, but it's not a guarantee. There's always the possibility that she'll find a real boyfriend—one who does more than get her off in bathrooms or laundry rooms.

The idea makes me panicky enough to consider cabbing it back to Waters', grabbing Lily and her things, and taking her back to my place. But I don't, because Miller's already looking at me like he's got something to say about the way I'm acting.

And honestly, even I get that I'm being a little weird about this whole thing. I just didn't expect my reaction to seeing Lily tonight, or hers to seeing me. Now all I can think about is getting her alone again so I can capitalize on all the naked time I'm planning to have with her this week.

I keep checking my phone while we're watching the game to see if Lily's as annoyed about this as I am, but there are no responses to my messages. She's having fun with the girls while I'm here with blue balls.

We're in a pretty private section, but we still don't go completely unnoticed. A couple of girls come over and start chatting up Lance, who's sitting across from me. I do my best to ignore them, but man, they're all over him, and he's tense as hell. Eventually he takes a phone number from one of them and sends them on their way. We're sort of trying to work by watching the game and planning strategy for when we play these teams.

"Not interested in bunny action tonight?" I ask.

"Action, yes; talking, no. If they're still here later, I'll get them to put their mouths to better use," Lance says.

He's not joking either. Some of the stories I've heard—both first and second-hand—about Lance's antics with the bunnies make my sex life seem weak. And it isn't.

By the time the first period is over, I'm resigned to the fact that it'll be a while before I can see Lily. This gives me more time to plan my attack when we get back to Waters' place. I know the layout of the bedroom we'll be staying in, since it's the one where we first had sex months ago, back in September. We have to make out in the bathroom at the very least, just for nostalgia.

I give up on staying sober and order a second pint, then a third. Near the end of the third period, Alex gets a call from Violet. It's not a regular call, though. Instead she FaceTimes him. She's clearly drunk, as I can hear her from the other end of the table. Her question filters down to me. *Jesus.* Is she asking about blow jobs? I hear a mention of *lollipopping*, and then Alex passes the phone to Miller with a shrug.

The game goes to commercial break, so I can hear better when Violet asks Miller if he likes blow jobs. Wow. Talk about open. I would never ask my sister that, mostly because I'd then want to murder the guy she was dating. It's probably a good thing she's halfway around the world and I can't police her boyfriends.

Miller's response is just as much an overshare, which Waters doesn't like. There's some wrestling over the phone and some reassurance from Violet that since Alex just admitted to liking blow jobs, it's hypocritical for him to be mad at Miller for saying the same thing. Miller's probably had a hell of a lot more women on their knees than Waters' has, but no one needs to point that out. Miller's caught enough flak over his not-so-pristine past with the bunnies; he doesn't need more.

Eventually the phone is handed to Lance and then to Westinghouse, who seems to have some fucked-up shit going on in the bedroom based on the content of his conversation. I try not to take the phone when he hands it to me, but I'm not left with much of a choice.

Violet's face comes into view. I'm mostly looking up her nose. She's sitting on the living room couch. I can hear the other girls in the background, but I can't see them. She takes a slurpy sip of her drink. "Balls." A hip thrust follows, and she sloshes wine over the rim of her glass. "Do you like blow jobs?"

I can't answer this question straightforwardly or honestly—not without sharing a lot more information than I'd like to. I run a hand through my hair and try not to think about my last blow job, which was an insanely long time ago. "They're all right, I guess."

Violet slow-blinks several times. "They're all right? *All right*? Are you telling me that having a woman's lips wrapped around your cock while you fuck her mouth doesn't do it for you?"

I have a sudden, vivid image of Lily on her knees with those incredibly luscious lips wrapped around my cock—me holding her hair, guiding that sweet, perfect mouth. It's quickly shattered when Waters dive bombs over Miller, nearly knocking over tables in his haste to get the phone out of my hand.

There's chastising from Waters and some laughter from Miller, but neither drowns out Lance's snarky comment: "Is this about your Frankenweiner, Ballistic?"

"Shut the fuck up, man!" This time it's my turn to launch myself at someone. And Lance is my target, even if he is at least twenty pounds heavier than I am. I knock over his pint, spilling beer on the table. His chair hits the ground with a loud bang as he jumps up to avoid the spill, and Westinghouse, who's sitting beside him, pushes back with a screech.

I take Lance in a headlock. "That's under the damn cone!"

"Get the fuck off me, asshole!" Lance punches me in the kidney.

I drop him, and he stumbles into another chair, knocking it over, too.

He charges me, face red, eyes wild—the way they get when someone rams into him on the ice. He slams his shoulder into my chest. He's like a damn bull. It's a good thing there's no one at the table beside us, because it almost goes over.

Miller grabs Lance by the back of the shirt and pulls him off me. "Calm the fuck down, you two. You're gonna get us thrown out."

"Stop touching me!" Lance shoves Miller's hand off and paces around in a circle, his head down as he breathes hard, rolling his shoulders.

Our waitress comes by to check on us and find out what all the commotion was about. Lance adjusts his shirt while Waters assures the waitress we're just playing around. Lance mutters an apology, and so do I.

When all the chairs are righted and we're sitting around the table again, Lance's brow furrows. He's still red-faced and agitated.

And I'm still pissed at him. "Thanks a lot, man. Lily didn't know about my fucked-up junk until now."

"Aren't you screwing her?"

Waters makes a sound from the other end of the table, like he disapproves of the terminology.

"Yeah."

"So she's gotta know about the accident then, aye?" Lance seems confused.

"I haven't told her about that." This is hella uncomfortable.

"What accident?" Westinghouse asks.

"Balls took a skate to the groin when he was a kid."

Both Waters and Westinghouse frown like they're trying to figure out what the big deal is.

"I wasn't wearing a cup," I supply to help them along.

Westinghouse's eyes widen. "Holy fuck."

"So, like—" Waters making a chopping motion.

"Yeah. Pretty much. But it's all still there, and it all still works. There's just a lot of scars."

There's some uncomfortable shifting as they put it all together.

"I still don't get it. So you do what? Make Lily blow you in the dark?" Lance asks.

Leave it to him to ask the questions I don't want to answer. Him and Violet. "She hasn't done that." I take a huge gulp of my beer.

There's silence around the table. I can feel their eyes on me.

"She doesn't like to suck cock?"

"She's offered. It's not really my thing." I've just told them far too much.

That gets me more strange looks, so I excuse myself to the bathroom so I can stop having this embarrassing and shitty conversation. I have some hang-ups about blow jobs, and I think my reasons are completely valid.

No one pushes me to talk more about it when I come back to the table, which is good. Lance has disappeared to the other side of the bar where those girls came from. He chats them up for a bit and gives us a wave when he's on the way out the door with both of them. Once the game is over, we settle the tab and head for the SUV.

Waters falls into step beside me. "You gonna crash at my place?"

"You cool with that?" If he's not, I'm calling a cab and taking Lily home with me.

"You're always welcome." He runs a hand through his hair. "Just be real careful with Lily. She hasn't had the easiest life, and she's a little…sheltered. I don't want to see her get hurt."

I almost choke on the *sheltered* part. I have a feeling Alex's perception of Lily is based on his high school memories, 'cause the woman who gets naked with me sure as hell doesn't act sheltered. I reserve my comment on that part and respond to the first statement. "I'm not gonna hurt her."

"I can't imagine you would on purpose."

There's a lot more space in the backseat since Lance isn't with us. I'm a little antsy, and the closer we get to Waters' place, the more anxious I become. The whole FaceTime conversation about blow jobs had to have started somewhere. Lord knows those girls are way worse than we could ever be with the shit they talk about.

Violet has zero filter, and who the hell knows what Westinghouse and Charlene get up to with that weird conversation tonight. I'm a little worried about the ideas those two may have put in Lily's pretty, clever head.

Lily's offered to kiss my dick on more than one occasion. Over the years I've perfected my excuses for why a blow job isn't a good idea—like, my dick will taste like latex, and then I won't be able to kiss her. Or I don't want to come in her mouth, or she can do that another time. Those work amazingly well. I then proceed with additional distractions, taking her mind off me and putting it back on her.

It's also never actually become a real issue, because I haven't hung out with anyone long enough for her to figure out there's more going on than me being super considerate.

I have an entire week with Lily, one in which I plan to have an excessive amount of sex. There's no fucking way I'm going to make it through a whole week without her seeing my dick. She'll want to shower with me. I'll want to have sex in the morning, the mid-morning, the afternoon. It can't always be dark.

It's going to be impossible to keep hiding this from her. And for the first time in my entire life since this shit happened to me, I'd actually like it if I didn't have to hide it. But if what happened the last time a chick got a load of my fucked-up dick happens with Lily …I think I might be wrecked all over again. I don't want to consider too closely what that means.

We pull into the driveway, and my anxiety kicks into high gear. The blue balls I've been rocking all night haven't gone away, but my dick is as limp as an overcooked noodle.

I'm the last one in the door, and I hang back, surveying the scene. Empty wine bottles litter the coffee table, along with takeout boxes. An abandoned Scrabble board sits in the middle, though I'm too far away to see the words.

All the girls have flushed cheeks. Lily's reclined on the couch in a pair of worn jeans and a T-shirt, heavy-lidded and loose-limbed. She smiles at me, and I return it, but all my worry on the ride here is suddenly amplified.

It doesn't take long before people start disappearing upstairs, and then it's just me and Lily. I'm so fucking nervous, and I don't even really know why. She's drunk for sure. I can dim the lights and make her feel good tonight. I'll worry about the rest later.

She's the one who comes up to me. She's the one who wraps her arms around my neck and whispers in my ear about going to prison. We've been bantering back and forth all week about pussy prison. Jesus Christ, do I ever want to go.

Lily takes my hand, her slightly fuzzy gaze questioning as she guides me up the stairs to the room we first fucked in. I'm slammed with all of those memories as soon as we step inside. That seems so long ago now. It's hard to believe it's already been five months. That's way longer than I usually let things go on with any bunny. But then Lily isn't a bunny, so the same rules haven't applied.

I hit the lights out of habit, snake an arm around her waist, and jump onto the bed with Lily facedown underneath me. I'm only sporting a semi, which is atypical when it comes to her, but I'm still distracted with trying to figure out how I'm going to manage the rest of the week, and how long I can get away with her not seeing the problem in my pants.

"Did you have fun with the girls tonight?" I ask.

Lily's giggling and breathless. "Uh-huh. Did you have fun with the boys?"

"I woulda rather been here with you. Or at my place with you," I say.

Her voice is soft and low when she responds. "I'm here with you now."

That she certainly is. I stretch out on top of her. She's all lean body and tight muscles. I stay there for a few long moments, just absorbing the feel of her under me.

When she turns her head to the side I sit back and find the hem of her shirt, pulling it over her head. Brushing her hair out of the way, I press a kiss to the nape of her neck. Her hair smells like the girly shampoo she uses, and her skin is salty and warm. I make a slow path down her spine with my lips, appreciating the soft hum I get in response on the way back up. Lily lifts her hips, pushing her ass against my erection.

"Randy?"

I make a noise rather than respond with words.

"Let me up."

"What?" For a second I think she's not interested in getting her fuck on with me.

"I want to turn over."

I exhale a relieved breath. Turning over I can handle. I prefer being able to see her face anyway. I push up on my arms, and she slithers out from under me in a rush. Maybe I was right about her lack of interest after all.

Except she unbuttons her pants, shimmying them down over her hips, along with her panties.

Or maybe I'm moving too slow.

Lily is naked.

Lily is perfect.

Lily is everything I want.

And she's right in front of me, yet all I can do is stare because I have no idea what the rest of this week is going to look like. I'm really fucking terrified that tonight is going to be the last night I get to be with her before she finds out I'm defective.

She slides her palms under my shirt, so I raise my arms to make it easier for her to take it off. Once I'm shirtless she runs her hands over my chest and circles my nipples. I groan, because the ache in my balls is back. Then she follows with her mouth. Jesus. I'm so fucking horny and stressed right now. There's too much going on in my head for me to be able to enjoy this the way I should.

All of a sudden I feel the soft brush of her fingers over the head of my cock. "Can I take these off?" She tugs on the waistband of my jeans. I let her, because the end result—getting naked—is what I've been waiting for, but when I try to pull her down to the mattress, she straddles me and pushes on my chest.

Lily isn't usually the aggressor.

"Randy?" Her voice is soft and breathless as her lips touch mine.

"Hmm?" I skim the gentle curve of her hip.

"I want your cock in my mouth."

There are things that happen that change a person's world. I'm pretty sure, looking back, this might be the moment I actually start to recognize that I have feelings for Lily extending far beyond what happens in my pants. And not because of the way she chooses to tell me she wants to blow me, but because of what follows that simple, yet powerful declaration.

Before we take this any further, I think it's important to go back in time for a few moments, to truly understand why it's so damn difficult to accept that Lily wants to wrap those gorgeous, luscious lips of hers around my cock.

My first—and last—failed attempt at getting a blow job happened when I was eighteen. That may seem old, but considering what I'd been through as a kid, and the fucked-up state of my dick, it hadn't seemed reasonable for me to test out the joys of the BJ before then. Up until I was drafted to the farm team, Miller and I had mostly hung out and watched highlights after games. He'd been getting tons of action from his tutors for a couple of years. My situation was a little different.

Sure, I whacked off all the time like normal guys my age, but I was highly aware that it took me a shitton longer to reach the end than it seemed to take others, even with all the practice I got. Everything worked, I just wasn't sure how well, and the few times I'd gotten handies from girls at parties in high school, it had been in the dark, fumbling around, and I'd always helped them out so I could finish. Sex was different. Even with a condom, all that hot and tight and wet made coming a lot easier. Also, naked girl and those soft noises—or loud ones—they made when they were getting close also helped.

I'd watched enough crappy porn to more than understand the allure of the blow job. Violet's graphic description of the act accurately depicts the exact reason why guys want to put their dick in a mouth. By that point I'd eaten out a couple of girls before we got down to the real business, too, so I got the allure of that. Having some girl writhing around underneath me, grabbing my hair and grinding herself on my face while I tongue-fucked her, was definitely hot. Plus I have a lot of dick, so I don't want to just get in there without any prep.

Anyway, on the night in question. I'd just finished doing that. The girl I was with—we'll call her Jezebel, even though that wasn't her name—had just come on a super-loud moan, thanks to my superior tongue skills. I'd already gotten a condom out and was ready to turn off the lights, drop my boxers, and roll that baby on. We'd been out a bunch of times, but it wasn't serious or anything, just a continual hook up.

However, apparently this time she wanted to return the favor.

I hit the lights before she straddled my legs and yanked my boxers down.

My eyes were already adjusting to the dark, so I could just make out the vague contours of her face. She was pretty with a nice body and she liked to fuck, so those were all pluses for me, at the time.

Then she engulfed the head. When she tried to take more, it was like an out of body experience. It was fucking awesome. Until the moment she stopped, shifted over and hit the light on the nightstand. Before I could think to react she was already heading back down.

And then she screamed. There is nothing that deflates a dick quicker than a girl's terrified scream, followed by the phrase, "What the fuck is wrong with your penis?"

There wasn't much of an opportunity to explain as she rushed around the room, grabbing her clothes and yelling about horror movies. It was dramatic. And obviously scarring, for both of us.

The rumors that followed sucked worse than the actual event, because they were blown way out of proportion. She tried to contact me a couple of years later to apologize, but I wasn't interested in hearing it.

After that I became incredibly proficient at mood lighting— and at getting the dick wrapped and where it was supposed to be before any girl had a chance to attempt to blow me. And on the occasions when an offer would come my way, all I had to do was think about the look on that girl's face and the way she couldn't get away from me fast enough to reconsider giving it another shot.

And now here's Lily, all sweet and gorgeous and unassuming, saying things to me that make me want to take her home and keep her forever. Which isn't possible. But we all have dreams.

"You don't need to do that," I tell Lily.

She bites her lip, looking uncertain. "I know, but I want to."

I'm prepared with one of my stock excuses. "It's really not

nec—"

"Please."

It's not just the way she says it, but the way she's looking at me—like if I say no it'll crush her—that makes me question exactly what I've been doing with her this entire time.

I glance over at the thin beam of light shining through the crack at the bathroom door. It's not dark enough in here to mask my problem. She must take my lack of response as an affirmative, because she starts kissing a slow trail down my stomach. When she reaches the waistband of my boxers, she stops and lifts her gaze. Eyes locked on mine, she presses a warm, wet kiss to the scar on my hip.

"I don't know if this is a good idea," I say.

She pushes my boxers down farther. "You think me sucking you off is a bad idea?"

Motherfuck.

When she says it like that, looking the way she does, with her face so close to where she's willing to put her mouth, it's hard to remember why this is such a terrible idea.

She doesn't yank off my boxers and start screaming, instead she runs the end of her nose along my erection through the cotton barrier. When she reaches the head, she peeks up at me and covers the fabric with her sweet mouth, sucking me through the barrier.

I ball my hands into fists and try to find the will to stop her, but I don't want to. Not yet. She repeats the same series of movements: the soft sucking through cotton, the brush of her nose and cheek along the shaft.

Next I feel the warm, gentle sweep of her fingers when she slips them into the pocket at the front of my underwear. At the same time, she pushes the waistband down and kisses the scar on my abdomen.

"Lily." I reach out, second-guessing how far I'm willing to let her take this.

She grabs my hand and bites my knuckle before she kisses it.

Then she licks my index finger and sucks it into her mouth. Her cheeks hollow out, and she makes that popping sound. She lays her cheek against my erection and looks up at me with soft, pleading eyes. "Please, Randy."

No one has ever begged to give me a blow job. No woman has ever looked at me the way she is right now, asking to give me something instead of looking to take.

I want this. I want her mouth. Not just because of the blow job—which I'm clearly interested in—but because I want her to want me regardless of whether I'm defective.

I slip a thumb into her mouth, and she swirls her tongue around it, showing me exactly what she plans to do to me. She pushes my boxers down until the head peeks out. Lily keeps her eyes on mine as she kisses the tip.

Her lips are so soft. I'm pretty sure my longevity will take a shot if she blows me, and I'm mostly okay with that. Then Lily engulfs the entire head and does an around-the-world with her tongue, adding some suction. It feels incredible. Like, out of this world.

I must make some kind of noise or say something, because she pops off and asks, "Is that okay?"

I nod, mostly because I'm worried if I use real words they're going to come out high-pitched and pre-pubescent sounding.

"I can do it again?" she asks, her lips sweeping the head as she speaks.

"Yeah. That'd be great."

She repeats the same lick, swirl, suck pattern a bunch of times before she tugs on my boxers. "I can take these off now?"

Only the head is exposed. If she takes my boxers off, she's going to see the mess under there. She nuzzles me and kisses the head again. She doesn't wait for a response, maybe because she knows I can't give her one.

"Eyes on me," she whispers.

She holds my gaze as she pulls my boxers down and keeps her lips on my skin. Eventually she has to look away, and when she does, I can see the moment she notices how prominent the scar is that runs from my right hip to my groin.

She looks up again and starts kissing her way across the scar. When her chin hits my cock, her gaze shifts down. I wait for her to push away, to have some kind of disgusted reaction to what she's seeing, because there's nothing hiding what's going on.

Instead she presses her lips to the heavy scar. "Does that feel okay?"

"Yeah." I say, hands still balled into fists.

Lily licks up the shaft, over the scars and back down again, slow and soft.

She keeps stroking me with her tongue, like she's eating her favorite kind of ice cream and doesn't want to stop. When she takes the head in her mouth and keeps going until it hits the back of her throat, I shove my hands in her hair.

It's exactly the image I had in my head earlier today. Except it's real.

"Okay?" Lily asks in a voice muffled by my cock in her mouth.

I stroke her cheek. "So fucking good."

I need to find a way to get Lily to move to Chicago, because this is a woman I don't want to be without.

SNEAK PEEK AND DELETED SCENE

There was one scene, that while I was writing it, I knew it wouldn't make it into the final cut, because it needed to be a little more serious than this pile of ridiculousness. I wrote it anyway, and figured I could share it the outtakes, along with the first chapter of *Forever Pucked*.

CHAPTER 1

VIOLET

Today is mine and Alex's one-year anniversary, and it sucks donkey dick. Well, it's one of our "anniversaries." Alex likes to celebrate every single milestone in our relationship because he's sappy and romantic like that. He also likes to have an excuse to buy me gifts. Lots of them. Extravagant ones. For my birthday he bought me a car. A nice car. With heated seats and automatic everything. New cars are scary because they don't have dings and dents, and they need to be maintained.

Anyway, I digress. Anniversaries. This month we're celebrating our "First Official Date" Anniversary. Alex likes to consider the first time we had sex our "real" anniversary, but since we hardly knew each other then, apart from how our genitalia fit together, I prefer to fast-forward a month to when I wasn't thinking with my beaver. Not totally, anyway.

It's still up for debate as to whether the day he locked me in the conference room at my work and forced me to have coffee with him later was our official first date. I'm inclined to go with the night he took me out for dinner and we ended up back at his place, banging on his couch, which is what we're celebrating tonight. It's marked on our calendar. There's even a sticker with a smiley face. I'm dubbing this one our *second sexiversary* because it's the second occasion when we had sex, and because it annoys Alex.

Sadly, we might not get the opportunity to fuck like it's our third time—we did it twice that first time, for those of you keeping score at home—again tonight. Alex is currently on a bus back to Chicago with the team after a series of four away games. He's been gone for more than a week. A snowstorm is blowing north through the Midwest, and last I heard from him, they were stuck at some rest stop—still more than two hours from home, and that's without the snow slowing them down.

It's already three in the afternoon. If they can't make it back before it gets dark and the storm picks up, he'll be stuck at a hotel for the night. We might be able to have phone sex, but that's not the same as hugging his wood with my beaver. So that's why this anniversary sucks.

And even *if* he makes it home tonight, he's bound to be bagged, which may put a damper on the sexiversary lovin'. Not that he won't perform. He will. He always does. But it won't be with the level of exuberance I've grown accustomed to over the past year. I might only get two orgasms out of him instead of the requisite three or four he usually strives for.

Charlene, my best friend and colleague at Stroker and Cobb Financial Management, peeks her head into my cubicle. She looks disembodied with the way the rest of her is out of sight. She's also smiling like she belongs in some kind of asylum.

"What's up?" I ask.

"You have a delivery."

"What kind of delivery?"

Alex likes to send me gifts at work. Once he had some guy dressed as a beaver sing a love song to me. It was mortifying. Jimmy, one of the other junior accountants, recorded it and posted it on YouTube. Obviously I made him take it down, but it had already gone viral.

"An Alex delivery."

I brace myself for humiliation as she grunts, moving my gift into view.

I don't say anything for a few long seconds. Alex is over the top with everything. But then, when you're the highest-paid NHL player in the league, you can afford to be extravagant and highly ridiculous.

"Not what you expected?" Charlene asks, biting her lip to keep from busting out laughing.

"What am I supposed to do with this?" I gesture to the four-foot stuffed beaver wearing a hockey jersey. It's almost as wide as it is tall. "I don't even know if it'll fit in my car."

I also don't want to carry it through the building.

"I'm sure we can make it fit." I ignore Charlene's eyebrow waggle. She's referencing my fiancé's monster cock. I'm not talking about a pet rooster, either. His dick is massive. I love it so much, even though putting it in my mouth is a workout all on its own.

I grab the beaver by its ears, hefting it into my cubicle so it's no longer blocking all the walking space between my office and the one across from me. Thank the lord Jimmy isn't in there or he'd be all over this. I need to hide the beaver. I don't have to see the back of the jersey to know it's got Alex's last name and number on it. This is a giant version of the small beaver Alex sent me back when he was first stalking me. Because I'm so awesome in bed. And he loves my boobs. And I told him I loved his cock. It was quite the first encounter.

My relationship with Alex Waters, center and team captain for Chicago, started as a one-night stand. A poorly thought-out one. I would've run into him after our night of passion since my stepbrother, Buck, is on his team, but I hadn't thought that far ahead when I was sticking my hands down his pants a year ago.

The beaver is holding a heart-shaped box. I pluck it from his paws while Charlene puts her arm around it and takes a selfie. I open the card; of course, it's beaver-themed—a pair of cartoon beavers with little hearts above their heads. They're in love, just like Alex and me.

I flip it open, expecting Alex's usual hilarity, which is how it starts, but by the end I'm about to cry. He really is that damn sweet:

Violet,

A year ago you agreed to go for coffee with me, and then your boobs agreed to go on a real date. You came into my life and turned it upside down in the best way. I'll never look at Spiderman pajamas the same way, or Marvel Comic boxer briefs.

I love every inch of you, all your funny quirky ways, all the ridiculous things you say in your sleep—and when you're awake. Your unending praise for the MC also doesn't hurt.

I know you don't buy the whole love at first sight thing, but I believe some people are destined to be together. Maybe we came together because of lust and Fielding, but we stayed together because of love.

You're my forever,
Alex

I sigh and hold the card to my chest, absorbing his words into my heart. Not really. I'm actually considering checking Google to see if he copied this from some sappy love poem site and made a few modifications to fit us better. However, Alex was an English major in college, so it's possible he came up with this all on his own.

I save the Google search for later and open the heart-shaped box. I expect to find chocolate inside, but I'm pleasantly surprised to discover it's filled with those heavenly maple sugar candies I love so much. There's also a bag of Swedish Fish.

"You two are the weirdest couple on the face of the earth. You know that, right?"

"I prefer the term *quirky*, but yeah, I know."

Charlene nabs a maple candy before I can close the box. Granted, there are a lot of them. If I had to hazard a guess, I'd say there's a good hundred candies in there. I'll be in a maple sugar coma by the end of the day for sure. I can't stop once I've started.

I grab my phone from the top drawer of my desk, but before I can pull up Alex's contact, Charlene snatches it out of my hand.

"What're you doing?"

"You need to pose with the beaver so we can send Alex a picture," she says, as if this should be obvious. Which really, it should be. I'm from the generation where everything we do gets posted online for bored people to see. Welcome to the wonderful world of well-documented bad decisions.

I shuffle the beaver around. It's not easy since he's huge, and my cubicle is small. I back my chair into a corner and move the beaver between my legs. I shove the beaver down so his head is at waist level, and Charlene snaps a few pics. Then we turn it over, giggling like idiots as I arrange my skirt over the top of its head so it looks like the beaver's going to town on my beaver.

I strike several different poses, including a fake orgasm face, which is the exact moment my boss walks in on our little party.

"Mr. Stroker! Hey, hi!" I push the beaver away from my crotch, but it's too late. He's already seen me molesting it.

"Miss Hoar." He glances at Charlene, then to me. "Miss Hall." His arms are crossed over his chest, and his face remote. He's giving away nothing. "You two look like you're hard at work."

We're in so much trouble.

"I'm so sorry, Mr. Stroker. Alex sent me this for our anniversary—" I gesture to the gigantic beaver. "—and Charlene and I thought we'd send a picture so he knows I got it. We're not sure if the team's going to make it back tonight, because of the storm." I wave my hand toward the windows. It's snowing like crazy.

Not that it's going to stop him from firing me.

"He sent you a stuffed woodchuck for your anniversary?"

"It's not a woodchuck; it's a beaver," Charlene says.

He raises an eyebrow. "I'm not sure I want an explanation. Violet, I'd like to see you in my office."

"Now?"

"Yes, now."

My stomach does a flip, but I stand and smooth out my wrinkled skirt, shooting Charlene a look of terror. She mouths *sorry* at me, but it's not her fault. I would've done something equally as stupid with or without her help.

I follow Mr. Stroker down the hall to his office. He closes the door behind me and gestures to the chair opposite his desk. I'm totally about to get canned. This is the shittiest sexiversary ever.

"I really am sorry about that, Mr. Stroker. We were being silly. I know it wasn't work-appropriate behavior."

He puts up a hand to stop me. "Violet, have you seen some of the clips Jimmy and Dean slip into their presentations? You doing whatever you were doing with that beaver has nothing on those two."

I know exactly what he's talking about. Jimmy and Dean are the other junior accountants at our firm. They're even more ridiculous than Char and me. Last week they threw a slide into their presentation with two hockey players mashed up against the plexiglas with the caption "Happy Hump Day!" It looked like there was a whole lot more than humping going on in the picture. And that's one of their tamer ones.

"Still, it won't happen again." I sag in the chair, unable to mask my relief. I honestly thought he was going to tell me to pack up my office. Then I'd be a famous hockey player's unemployed fiancée rather than a modest financial contributor to our partnership.

"Sounds good."

Mr. Stroker shuffles account files around on his desk. I

recognize the one on top as one I prepared, because it's in a violet-colored folder. Alex bought them for me. He thinks they're cute.

"I've reviewed your file for the Darcy account. I think you've made some very wise choices in terms of the funds you've selected. The returns have been high in the past eighteen months, and you've balanced their portfolio well."

"Oh. Well, thanks." This isn't at all what I thought I was coming here for. His praise is unexpected. He's a numbers guy, like so many of us in this department. It's always about the bottom line: whether or not we're making money for our clients or saving their asses from potential bankruptcy.

Mitch Darcy plays defense for Chicago. I met him through Alex. One night after the game his wife was there, and we started talking. She asked what I did for a living, so I told her. She seemed surprised that I worked a job other than servicing Alex's amazing dick.

Two weeks later, Mrs. Darcy made an appointment and specifically asked for me. Mr. Stroker took a risk by letting me draw up a proposal for the account. Of course he has to review it before anything can be implemented, but it's an opportunity I wouldn't have without all my connections. Those sometimes make me unpopular at work.

"This is a big deal, Violet." Mr. Stroker says, tapping his pen against the folder.

"Yes, sir."

"You're aware that Darcy renewed his contract for five more years at four million a year."

"Yes, sir. He also has endorsements with Power Juice and Sports Mind totaling another two million annually for the next three years."

"Do you think you'll be ready to present this to the Darcys next week?"

I sit up straighter. "You want me to present?"

"His wife is rather insistent it be you."

"But I've never presented to a client this big before."

"You've been managing Miller's account for the past year without an issue," he argues.

Stroker is referring to my stepbrother, Buck, whose real name is Miller. Everyone has recently started calling him by his given name, but it's an adjustment for me. I'm not quite there yet.

Usually the accounts I handle are half a million or less. The Darcys' portfolio is far more significant. Way bigger than anything I've touched, apart from Buck's accounts, and I've always had Mr. Stroker look at those before I make any kind of change. I don't want to be responsible for screwing up Buck's fortune.

"You've got a handle on it. Why don't you call them and set up a meeting for next week. I'm open most mornings."

"Okay, great. I'll consult their game schedule and see what works best."

"Perfect. You arrange it, check the notes I've made on the PowerPoint, and at the end of the week—say, Friday afternoon—I'll set aside an hour and you can do a dry run for me so you feel prepared. How does that sound?"

"That sounds amazing, Mr. Stroker."

"It's just William, Violet. You can drop the formality now."

He's told me this before, but I find his last name entertaining. "Of course. Right, William."

He gives Randy Balls, another one of Alex's teammates, a run for his money with the dirty names.

"Great. Three o'clock Friday afternoon is open for me. Book the conference room with Edna on your way out." He passes over the folder and picks up the phone, which means I'm dismissed.

I thank him and stop to set things up with his assistant on the way back to my cubicle.

Charlene is sitting at her desk, chewing her nails and pretending to do some kind of research. When she sees me she grabs my arm and yanks me into her cubicle. "Why aren't you crying? Didn't you get fired?"

"No. Stroker didn't can my ass."

Charlene sighs with relief. "I'm so sorry. He rarely comes down this way." It's true. Junior accountants usually only see the boss-man in the conference room on meeting Monday, which was this morning. "Let's never take pictures like that again while we're at work."

"Agreed. We should have waited until I got home. Then we could've posed the beaver on the bed so it looks like he's taking me from behind, or holding my boobs."

"Such good ideas. So what did Stroker say?"

"I'm presenting to Mitch Darcy and his wife next week."

"You're what?" she practically screeches this, so anyone within earshot, which is most of the office, peeks their head over the edge of their cube wall.

"It's okay, everyone. I told Charlene I'm thinking about going vegan."

Jimmy seems to have returned from his coffee break. He looks suspicious, and rightfully so—I'm the first one to order a Philly cheesesteak when he gets takeout—but he's on the phone, so he goes back to his call. The rest of the office is used to our ridiculousness, so they resume whatever they were doing, too.

I lower my voice to a whisper. "I get to present."

"That's a big account," Charlene whispers back.

"I know."

"That's amazing."

I know she means it, but I recognize the wistful look in her eyes. We're close, but we're still competing with each other, and with Jimmy and Dean, for a senior accountant position when it comes open. Being allowed to present to one of the bigger clients gives me an advantage over everyone else.

The people who don't like me at the office are really going to hate me now.

FOREVER PUCKED DELETED SCENE

THE PERFECT PLACE FOR BUDDY

"Maybe we should just elope." I'm not sure if it sounds like I'm kidding or not.

Violet lifts her head, her eyes wide. "You're kidding, right?"

I tuck strands of wet hair behind her ear and trace the line of her jaw. "I don't have to be."

"I don't have a dress."

I follow the contour of her bottom lip with my thumb. Jesus, I love this woman. "We can buy you one."

"You're serious?"

"As serious as you are about keeping me out of your Area 51."

Violet sits up. She's wearing a hotel robe. It gapes in the front and most of her right boob falls out. "I'm only mostly serious about that."

"What? You mean you'd let me in there?" I sit up, too, and stick my hand in the gap in her robe, palming a breast, ready to make all of my fantasies come true.

"Hold on there, trigger." Violet puts a hand on my face and pushes me back down. "I don't mean with the Super MC. He's huge. And there's special lube and stuff for that, which we don't have. I mean maybe we can use some more fingers, or, like, a toy—eventually."

108

"That'd be a great place to put Buddy…" That's exactly where I'd like to see that fucking dildo go. I would derive so much satisfaction, in so many ways, from watching that stupid beaver face disappear inside her ass.

"Wow. You're totally serious about that. I honestly don't understand the fascination with trying to get something that big into a hole that small." She pokes my hard-on.

"That *is* the fascination, Violet."

"You know, I've done some reading recently about this."

"Oh, really?" I lean against the headboard. "And what did you discover?"

"You're the one with the prostate gland, not me. So if anyone should be putting things where the sun don't shine, it should me giving you a dose of Buddy, not the other way around." She crosses her arms over her chest and cocks a brow.

"Uh, yeah, that's not going to happen. Ever, Violet."

She shrugs. "That's fine. But if you won't let me try it on you, then you don't get to try it on me."

"Okay."

"That's it? Okay? You're not going to argue over this?"

"Baby, c'mere." I pat my lap.

Violet doesn't straddle me, but she sits on my hard-on, so that's okay. I tilt her chin up. "Do you remember what I said to you the first night we met?"

"Am I looking at her beaver?"

I smile. "Later. When we were in my suite, and we ended up in the bedroom."

"It isn't that big—which is lie, because it really is *that* big." She shifts so her ass rubs against my still-growing dick.

"No. I mean just before that."

She bites her lip and thinks for a few seconds, playing with the hair at the nape of my neck. "Oh!" Her smile is soft, shy almost. "That we didn't have to do anything I didn't want to. But you had to know at that point I was going to give it up for you."

109

"Well, I hoped, but it was never an expectation. I mean, fuck—I really wanted to get you naked and get all up in there, but I would've been perfectly fine with some slip 'n' slide or the blow job. The sex was—" I close my eyes, remembering exactly how being inside Violet for the first time felt. So tight, so hot, so... "—much more than I probably deserved at the time."

"I was pretty nervous."

"I was, too. I'm not really a one-night-stand guy."

Her smile is warm. "You got attached to my beaver rather quickly."

"Mmm." I sweep her hair over her shoulders and push the robe down with it. "And the rest of you."

I slip an around her waist and pull her closer so I can kiss her. "What I'm trying to say, Violet, amidst all these distractions, is that I will only take from you what you offer me willingly, and only if it's going to make you feel good. And that goes for everything."

"I love you. But all your sweet-talking still isn't going to get the Super MC Area 51 access."

ABOUT THE AUTHOR
HELENA HUNTING

NYT and USA Today bestselling author of PUCKED, Helena Hunting lives on the outskirts of Toronto with her incredibly tolerant family and two moderately intolerant cats. She's writes contemporary romance ranging from new adult angst to romantic sports comedy.

CPSIA information can be obtained
at www.ICGtesting.com
Printed in the USA
LVOW04s2038061016
507643LV00001B/8/P